HE HAS MANY NAMES

DREW CHIAL

Cover by Matthew Revert

ISBN: 978-1-944866-22-8

CLASH Books

PO BOX 487 Claremont, NH 03743

"When you spit into an abyss, the abyss spits back."

- Friedrich Nietzsche, *Beyond Good and Evil*

...sort of

TABLE OF CONTENTS

THE ORALIA

I'D BEEN TRYING to get ahold of my agent for months. I was beginning to think she was dead. Then she called, at dawn, sounding like she'd run up a flight of stairs. "Noelle, drop whatever you've got going on tonight."

Box wine and ramen, done.

"A publisher wants to meet with you at the Oralia Hotel. It's super swanky and upscale. So doll yourself up."

I hung up and spent more time putting my pitch together than my outfit. I got ready at the eleventh hour, ruined a zipper in my panic, and did my makeup in a series of swift strokes right before my Uber pulled up.

I scooted into the middle seat nervously adjusting my necklace in the mirror. It was a bib of emerald laurels mom had given me for just such an occasion. I have no idea how much it set her back, but it was priceless on waitress's salary. And...I had it on backward. I unlatched the bib, flipped it around, and struggled to get it back on.

"You know what you look like with your good bag and cheap shoes?" I muttered in my best Hannibal Lecter voice. "You look like a rube."

"What was that?" My driver squinted through the mirror.

"I was just wondering if you could go a little faster."

• • •

The Oralia was hard to pick out of the skyline. Its bricks were so black it blended into the storm, but there was no missing the hotel when facing it dead on. Spotlights shot up the columns, like something off the poster for a silent film. The entrance was made of dark marble tiles separated by a grid of gold. A golden maze-like pattern ran up the side of the building. The balconies started on the third story.

I walked inside and a bellhop stepped forward. "Welcome to the Oralia. May I take your things?"

I handed him my umbrella and kept my briefcase to myself.

I strode past chandeliers that looked like pipe organs, gorgeous gargoyles, and a giant clock that assured me I didn't have time to appreciate the art deco architecture.

It felt like I was rushing through the set of a Busby Berkeley film. Big buxom sculptures grazed my case, water fountains sprayed my forearms, and ballroom music beckoned me in.

The archway between the lobby and the check-in counter featured a gilded recreation of the entrance: a skyscraper lit from the bottom up. Behind the front desk was a smaller version of the same thing.

From the stained glass stars to the bright red carpeting, the lobby screamed Golden Age Hollywood. Even the name Oralia meant golden. I felt certain that this was one of the last bastions of elegance and class from an era when there was still tinsel in tinsel town.

I scanned the plaque on the counter to confirm my suspicions.

And...the hotel was founded in 2008.

The concierge didn't notice me. She was face deep in a paperback. I leaned over to see what it was. I couldn't catch the title, but I caught the hunk of beefcake on the cover.

At this stage of my career in publishing I was in the retail sector, working at an establishment whose name rhymes with Yarns and Global. The hardest part of my job was when I had to tear the covers off of the romance novels that weren't selling. The publishers didn't want them. They just needed to know we weren't giving them away, so they had us send back the remains. I felt bad for the male models on the covers, all their bench presses gone to waste. I felt worse for the women on the back, smiling with their eyes so full of hope, yearning to be loved.

I daydreamed writing romance under a penname, giving single women the bearded billionaire bondage experience of their dreams. I'd like to say it was artistic pride that kept me from doing it, but really, it was fear of not being able to pull it off. Romance wasn't my area of expertise.

The concierge felt my eyes on her. She buried her guy-candy in a drawer, folded her spectacles, and stood up.

"May I help you?"

I gave her a nervous smile. "I'm here to see Matilda MacDonald."

The concierge pointed to a vampish figure on a couch in the corner.

Matilda wore a black pants suit that was all pleats and leather, with no undershirt. The Pradas she'd kicked up on the footrest were patent leather with heels that went on forever. She wore her jet-black hair in a pixie cut. Topping off her look was an armored ring that ran the length of her index finger.

Matilda swiped at a phone in an embroidered leather case. In her clutches, it looked like a forbidden text filled with spells for calling up the dead.

I extended my hand. "Matilda MacDonald?"

Matilda extended the hand with the armored ring. "Noelle Blackwood. It's a pleasure to finally meet you."

I held my briefcase to my chest. "The pleasure is mine. Publishers never reach out to mid-listers. Who do I have to thank for floating my name in your direction?"

Matilda smirked and took her seat. She reached into her bag and slid a book across the table. "I trust you've heard of Barkley Carver."

Barkley Carver, his name always made me think of trees, especially since there were evergreens on the covers of all of his books, including this one *Out on a Limb*.

Cover artists used tree lines as visual shorthand for shallow graves, which fit since all of Barkley's stories started with hikers discovering a body. Barkley filled his fictitious funeral plots with the segment of the populace that made up his audience: upper-class white women; the same ones the media turned into saints whenever they went missing, say while jogging through the woods. This is why the mystery section of every bookstore looks like a forest mural.

Barkley took this theme a step further by working it into each of his titles: *Fruit from the Poison Tree*, *Shake Like a Leaf*, and *A Tree Falls Silent*.

I flipped the book over to find the same portrait Barkley Carver had used for the last twenty years. The author stood proud in his bomber jacket, full flight suit, and helmet. He leaned on the nose of a fighter jet and looked to the sky in big aviator shades.

Matilda signaled to the bellhop. He set a storage bin on the table, and flipped it open.

I peered inside. "What's that for?"

Matilda nodded at my luggage. "Your briefcase, your coat, your phone, and a smart watch if you have one."

I tapped my luggage. "What about my manuscript?"

Matilda drew a piece of paper from beneath the table. “Think of this meeting as less of an acquisition and more of a commission. Go ahead put it in.”

“Then I suppose you’ll want my Wi-Fi glass eye and fiber optic hair extensions?”

Matilda rolled her eyes. “Would you be so kind?”

Joking aside, Matilda wasn’t going to pass anything my way until I gave up my phone, so I did, and the bellhop left with the bin.

Matilda slid the piece of paper across the table. It wasn’t an offer. It was a nondisclosure agreement. I skimmed far enough to get to the part where I realized Matilda’s proposition wouldn’t start until I’d signed.

I drew a squiggle and slid the agreement back. “Why all the secrecy?”

Matilda swapped the agreement for a manila folder. “This offer is for you alone. Barkley and I, we’re not like other publishers. We don’t take submissions. We seek out talent and your name, Noelle, has come up several times. Your screenplay for *The Identity Thieves* just made the blacklist. Script readers gave it their highest marks, but do you know why it will never get made into a film?”

I shrugged. “Because it doesn’t have the words ‘fast’ or ‘furious’ in the title?”

Matilda nodded. “Because it can’t be retooled to fit an existing franchise, yes, just like your first manuscript couldn’t be softened into teen lit, and your last one couldn’t be sold as fantasy or horror. Your work defies traditional branding. Now that’s where we come in.”

I shook my head. “What is it with the royal we? I thought you only published Carver’s titles.”

“Oh we do, but we publish 5 Carver titles a year. We’d like to ratchet that number up to 15.”

“Those are James Patterson numbers.” I slouched into the

sofa with an underwhelmed sigh. This was all starting to make sense. "You want me to ghostwrite for Carver. You know, serial killer thrillers aren't really my forte."

Matilda leaned forward and tented her fingers. "Barkley chose you because he wants to explore a new direction."

I cocked my head. "He's read my work?"

Matilda pushed her armored ring back and forth. "You know that paranormal investigations podcast you're on?"

Ohhh. "So he's heard my work."

"We've listened to all nineteen episodes."

"Then you know I'm just the token skeptic, there to make the show seem balanced."

"Maybe that's why they hired you, but you're the star of the show. Every week you break down all of their supernatural pseudo science into simple psychology."

Turning a screw into my skull, I quoted myself. "Stimulate the anterior insula and you too can see a ghost."

"Have you?"

"Of course. We're hardwired to see faces everywhere."

Matilda raised an eyebrow. "Seriously?"

"I've seen them in wallpaper, marble tiles, even a chain length fence when the light hit it just right."

Matilda cocked her head. "And you never flinched?"

I shrugged. "Our ancestors had to spot predators in an instant. So sometimes we see face where there are none, the Virgin Mary on toast or a cloud shaped like Donald Trump. It's just a glitch in evolution."

Matilda nodded recognizing this talking point from the podcast. "People don't hallucinate that much, do they?"

I nodded. "Oh yeah. No need for drugs or schizophrenia. With enough anxiety people will see all sorts of things."

Matilda leaned forward. "Are you speaking from experience?"

"About anxiety or hallucinations?"

Matilda tilted her head back and forth.

"On the podcast, when I said part of my writing ritual involved speaking to my characters like they were actually there—"

Matilda perked up. "*Walk ins* you called them; imagined figures that felt like they were literally in the room."

"I was being hyperbolic to prove my point."

Matilda feigned a smile. "Still, you're clearly qualified for this, so much so that Carver is eager to lend you his name."

I looked down at my boots, still wet from the walk. "Yeah, but isn't that cheating?"

"It's collaborating. He's the architect. You're the engineer. He draws the blueprints. You build the house."

"And how extensive are Carver's blueprints?"

Matilda tapped the manila folder with her pen. "He's written a ten-page synopsis."

"So it's a sketch on a bar napkin?" Matilda shrugged. "It's bare bones, but think of how much freedom that'll give you."

I waved my hands in the air. "Yeah, but it's Carver's name on the building. How does that help my career?"

Matilda leaned forward. "Right now, your name, with your following in the paranormal community, might get you into a local bookstore. Carver's name will get you that prime checkout counter space at a national grocery chain."

"Were you a real estate agent prior to your career as a publisher?"

"I've been many things." Matilda smiled and passed the manila envelope across the table. "This one little book will earn you royalties for the rest of your life. It'll buy you time to get your own *magnum opus* in print."

I shuddered. "I could always put it out myself."

Matilda pursed her lips, feigning optimistic approval. "It's true, as a group, self-publishers are taking bigger bites out of the e-book pie, but as individuals most of you are starving.

Anonymous reviews don't have the sway of syndicated columns, podcasts don't have NPR's listeners, and trendsetters don't have the influence of traditional publishers. Go ahead and throw your book at the wall, see if it sticks, but when readers have so many options they prefer established brands."

I unbuttoned the top button of my blouse and let out a low sigh. "How does this bestseller factory of yours work?"

Matilda raised her eyebrow, knowing she had me.

"You'll stay here, in the Oralia, until you've finished a draft. We'll comp the room, the pay-per-view," she tilted her head back and forth, "and room service within reason."

I looked toward the concierge. "Why put me up here? Doesn't Carver trust anyone to keep his secret?"

Matilda bit her lip to conceal her smile. "It's something new we're trying. Think of yourself as an artist in residence. The Oralia isn't old, but it was built by people who remember when this town was filled with magic. Soak it in."

I scanned the lobby of the creepy hotel that was to be my home.

"This is starting to sound a lot like a Stephen King story, one that didn't end well for the author in it. Is there any kind of advance?"

Matilda produced an attaché case and took her time entering the combination.

The locks clicked open and she slid the case across the table. It was lined with stacks of cash. They were twenties, but more money than I'd ever seen.

Matilda slammed the case shut. "This will be in a safe behind the counter. Send us a draft in one month and management will be authorized to hand it over."

"One month?"

"It's how Carver wants it done. It's in the contract. Think of it as a writing marathon."

I reflected on my first semiautobiographical novel. I

labored on it in my twenties, sold it for pennies, and watched it barely make back the advance.

I looked back at the cash. "All that for one month's work?"

Matilda nodded.

"When can I check in?"

Matilda slid another document across the table. "Right after you sign on the dotted line."

•••

The bellhop led me across the lobby. He had a classic uniform. Lopsided brimless cap, fitted coat, and bowtie. His sharp lanky features made him seem young, but his steel stubble, crooked nose, and distant gaze said something different. He wasn't cute, he was handsome. He pressed the call button for the elevators without so much as glancing in my direction.

Like the archway in the lobby, the sculpted surface of the doors resembled the Oralia's entrance.

"I sense a motif."

The bellhop nodded. "Retro future. They wanted to evoke a Hollywood that never really was." He spread his hands as he recited from a script, "A vision of the city through a glass darkly."

When the doors opened, I was startled at the sight of myself staring back at me. I stepped onto a neon grid and into an elevator made of mirrors, a Narcissus's wet dream, a living hell for anyone with body image issues.

The bellhop hit the button without announcing the floor number or acknowledging my reflection. I got the sense that he'd trained himself to do this for the guests' comfort, but it only made things more awkward.

"Have you ever heard of The Devil's Toy Box?" I asked.

The bellhop shook his head.

"There was a shack, out in the sticks, with mirrors from

floor to ceiling. Legend had it if you stood there for too long the Devil came to claim your soul."

"You realize I go up and down these elevators every day?"

"So you know?"

"So now I'm going to be thinking about that all the time."

I put my hands up. "It's just an urban legend, a rural legend really, a backwoods barn folk legend if I'm being honest."

"You're describing where I came from."

My eyes bulged and my chin vanished into my neck. So that's what I looked like with my foot in my mouth. I tried to face away, but the mirrors made that impossible. The awkward silence lasted for several floors.

I gave the bellhop another nervous smile. "We're going pretty high. Did Carver spring for the Princess Suite?"

The bellhop cocked his head. "Not exactly."

The elevator dinged on the 19th floor, second from the top.

ROOM 1901

SOMETHING JUTTED out from Room 1901. It had curled horns, pointed ears, and a long beard. It was gnawing on a big brass knocker.

I pointed to it. "Speak of the Devil."

The bellhop unlocked the door.

I squinted, curious. "Why would you put a knocker on a hotel door, unless this room was some kind of..."

He flipped the lights on.

"... sex dungeon..."

The 19th floor of the Oralia was where they kept the fantasy suites. This one had a forest theme, because of course it did. There was a mural wrapping around the walls, filled with a mix of saplings and old growth trees. The shortest were knee high while the tallest were as big as towers.

Tree trunks ran from the floor to the ceiling in lieu of support beams. The bark had been shellacked to give the impression the trees were wet, branches made the loft look like a forest canopy, rubber ivy leaves dangled from the ceiling. Oh, and of course the carpet was green.

"There is no way this room is up to fire code."

The bellhop shook his head. "I've been assured it is."

The countertop was a long slab of redwood with a knotted surface, with swirling grains, and rustic edges. The tables were stained stumps on hairpin legs, and the lamps were patchworks of driftwood.

"If Carver really wanted me to go all Ralph Waldo Emerson, why didn't he just spring for a cabin?"

The bellhop set the crate filled with my belongings on the coffee table. "I don't know, but I guarantee this suite has amenities you're not going to find in any cabin."

I honed in on the sex swing at the center of the parlor. Its chain was covered in a soft green grip lined with leaves and rubber grapevines. I couldn't help but push it toward the bellhop. He watched it swing without saying a thing. I kept pushing and giggling, until he cracked the slightest of smiles and pushed it back.

"Like this for instance."

The bedroom had everything you'd expect from a hotel, just in shades of green and brown.

The bellhop flipped a switch and the end tables lit up. He pointed to the lamps. "These are here if you want to get some work done, but if you really want to get the full experience, there's this."

He dimmed the lamps, flipped the next switch, and pointed up. There was a big round lantern in the corner of the room. Its shade was textured like the lunar surface. This moon shaped lamp gave the space a soft eerie glow. The rest of the ceiling was covered in a thousand fiber optic lights, scattered at random like stars in the night sky.

"I want that," I said, staring at it.

The bellhop nodded. "I want to take it home and stick a little flag in it."

"I know, right."

In this light, the bellhop's naturally squinting eyes,

crooked nose, and greying stubble made him look distinguished.

His eyes widened. "Oh, you're going to love this."

He directed me back into the hall.

The wall facing the bedroom was covered in prop rock surfacing. The door was curved like the entrance to a cavern. He opened it, flipped a switch, and lit a row of oil lanterns with fake LED flames.

The sink sat in a floating redwood counter, filled with an assortment of potions, lotions, and jellies. The mirror was framed in driftwood. Inside there was a Jacuzzi shaped like a hot spring, a toilet made of granite, and a toilet paper dispenser made of antlers.

He directed my attention to the Styrofoam stalactites. He turned a nozzle and a waterfall poured through a sinkhole.

I was struggling to see how any of this was erotic. The suite was impressive, but the kid in me still wished it had a ball pit.

I walked through the hallway and back into the fake forest. "All this plant life and no natural light?"

The bellhop trailed behind. "The guests want privacy."

I spun around. "From what, the Jolly Green Giant?"

"Drones."

I raised an eyebrow. "Seriously?"

He was dead serious. "Look out the balcony and you'll see them hovering."

He pointed to a shiny spot in the mural. There was a trail painted on the outside of a pair sliding glass doors.

"The paparazzi follow celebrities up to the entrance and minutes later those things are circling the building. I actually hit one with a broom."

"Did you knock it down?"

He patted his bicep. "Oh yeah, but they keep coming back."

It occurred to me that Barkley Carver might be one such

celebrity the drones had tried to capture mid-coitus. I had an unpleasant image of him, with his wrinkled brow and hangdog jowls, mounting an avid fan in that vine swing. In my vision, Carver was gritting his teeth, hammering away, wearing nothing but his aviators and a smile.

I shook that image out of my head. "Did Ms. MacDonald say anything about sending up some clothes or basic amenities?"

"You didn't pack any?"

"I didn't know I was checking in."

He stroked his chin. "There's some Oralia Apparel in the gift shop: sweatpants, pullovers, nothing fancy."

"Anything in the way of undergarments?"

"Uh...it's kind of lacking in that department," he answered awkwardly, glancing nervously at my chest, quickly averting his gaze.

... And now he was picturing me naked. I'd said *undergarments* and my body was flashing through his mind in every yoga pose, in every Kama sutra position. Men have an uncanny talent for visualization, which is why I didn't feel bad about doing the same thing to him, scanning his broad shoulders down his abdomen, picturing the V of his hipline. What? He started it.

Still, it was nice knowing I could make a man blush and there was something about this one, a warmth. I felt a strange pull back toward that swing.

I made a show of tugging at the overgrowth that ran down the wall. "I guess I could fashion something from these vines."

The bellhop smirked. "Would you like me to order some things, charge them to the room?"

I cupped my hands together. "Would you be so kind?"

"No problem. It would be a far cry from some of the weirder items I've had to deliver. Was there a particular style you'd prefer?"

I shrugged. "I'll take sports bras or boxers, really, I'm not picky."

He tilted his head, realizing he'd probably need a little more information.

I found a pen and jotted some details on a page of hotel stationary. "Oh and you'll want my measurements."

"Um," he stammered, fidgeting his hands, though he remained standing straight, like one of those guards at Buckingham Palace.

I handed him the page. "For the order."

"Yes, of course. Anything else I can help you with?"

I made a pair of right angles, with my fingers, and spread them over the forest. "Not unless you can find me a story."

"The room does have some history."

"Since 2008?"

"Oh yeah."

All right, he'd piqued my interest. "Rock and roll suicide, traveling serial killer, Scientology scandal?"

The bellhop's face indicated that I was only getting colder. "Pornography, actually. It's on your pay-per-view if you want to see."

I didn't immediately shake my head. "Is it safe to eat off of the counters?"

He nodded. "The room has been thoroughly sanitized, yes." And on that note, he presented his nametag. "If you need anything, just call the front desk and ask for Stephen, with a PH."

"Like Stephen King?"

"Or Stephen Colbert."

"That's a good name to have." I have no clue why I said that, or why I punctuated it with a knowing look, like I was Lauren Bacall saying some well-timed innuendo, but I did.

Stephen bowed out of the room with a similar look on his face, happy to see he could still make a woman blush.

BARKLEY'S NIGHTMARE

WHEN I STEPPED out of the Jacuzzi, I understood the value of luxury. All of my reservations about staying in the Oralia were massaged away in that heavenly tub. The room was misty with steam.

I put on a robe, put up my hair, and tore into Barkley Carver's packet, spilling his notes across the bed.

There was a letter written on aged parchment with something clipped to the back.

I unfolded it.

I heard the door creak open as my imagination invited Barkley in. He marched down the hall in his bomber jacket, flight suit, and helmet. This projection of Barkley wore his pilot's license like a fashion statement. Despite what I told Matilda, this was a normal part of my process. Characters walked in and out of my life all the time. It's why I never wrote in public, because I hadn't figured out how to pull it off without talking to myself.

We exchanged a nod of acknowledgement.

"Barkley."

"Noelle."

Then Barkley read over my shoulder.

Dear Noelle,

Thank you for accepting my invitation and my challenge.

"And your payment." I added.

Matilda has instructed the staff to keep tabs on your movements. You are not to leave the Oralia until you've submitted a draft. If you step foot off of the premises before the end of the month you forfeit the advance.

"Then technically it's not an advance."

Stay and you'll be given a per diem to spend in the hotel. Buy whatever the Oralia has to offer, just know that the card will be flagged if items from your Amazon wish list show up. This isn't for that.

I sifted through the pages on the bed until I found the card. "Hell-o."

I know what you're thinking, and the answer is: no, I do not usually sequester my writers. This is a unique situation. It has nothing to do with my confidence in you, and everything to do with the room you're staying in.

You see I stayed in that room on my second honeymoon--

I gave myself a moment to let that visual come and go.

--and I had a terrifying encounter.

I put a finger to Barkley's lips. I held the letter to my forehead like Johnny Carson playing at psychic. "You had your first experience with sleep paralysis and now you believe the room is haunted."

I unfolded the letter so Barkley could continue.

I woke up in the middle of the night, only I couldn't move, some unseen presence was holding me down.

"And they call my stories 'predictable.'"

I went back into the parlor and plopped down on the sex swing. Leaves rustled overhead. I put my feet up and arced my legs until I got a good pendulum motion going.

Barkley followed. He pushed me as he recalled his experience.

A cool breeze rolled through the room. Wood creaked all around. I sensed movement in the forest mural on the walls, until I realized the walls were gone.

I couldn't sit up or turn my neck, but I could shift my gaze. I looked at Mona, she and the mattress were gone and the green carpeting had turned into grass.

I'd fallen asleep in downtown LA and awoken in an old growth forest like the one that surrounded my childhood home.

I was overwhelmed with the sense that I was not alone. A shadow weaved in and out of the trees. It stretched up the trunks and ducked back into the dark. Its shape became clearer as it drew nearer.

I held the letter to my forehead. "Let me guess, it bore an uncanny resemblance to the knocker on the door."

It had horns, hooves, and a tail, but it walked upright like a man. When he stepped out of the shadows, the shadows came with him. The silhouette towered over me, a dream demon made of darkness.

I spoke over my shoulder to Barkley. "The clinical term for what you experienced is a *hypnopompic hallucination*. People suffering from sleep paralysis often dream with their eyes open. It's like sleepwalking in reverse. The reason the figure looked like a shadow is because that's one of the easiest shapes for your mind to form."

I added, "Do your research," in my best British accent.

This was why Barkley hired me. Any hack could write a jump scare, but I knew enough about the psychology to trick readers into believing me.

Barkley continued.

The demon's tail wagged between his legs, his head bobbed back and forth, and his eyes glowed red with a swirling maelstrom of flame. Plumes of steam rolled off his hairline.

"Plumes, Carver? Were you attacked by a smokestack?"

The demon crouched, crawled forward, and pressed his cheek to mine. His beard felt like steel wool, his flesh felt like ash, and his lips felt like leather against my ear.

He whispered, "I can smell your soul."

I examined the postcard clipped to the back of the letter. It was a print of Henry Fuseli's famous oil painting *The Nightmare*.

In it a goblin squatted on a maiden's chest, while a horse peeped on from behind a curtain. This was textbook sleep paralysis. Carver was new to horror. He had no idea this image had graced a dozen book covers.

I unwrapped the towel from my hair as my vision of Carter paced the room rubbing his shoulders.

I was so shaken by this nocturnal visitation I spent the next morning drafting an outline. Reviewing it, I realized none of the authors I've worked with were qualified to flesh it out. Their backgrounds were in law enforcement, forensics, and profiling. Demonology was outside their field of study.

I thought about taking it on myself, but I didn't want this story rattling around my brain while I slept. Serial killers I can deal with. Serial killers are the products of circumstances and genetics, but the Devil, true spiritual evil, that's a responsibility I'd rather pass on.

That's where you come in, Ms. Blackwood. You roll your eyes at the things that go bump in the night, you stare into the void without flinching. That is why I'm inviting you to apply your penchant for horror fiction to my outline, in the very room that inspired it... If you dare.

Regards,
Barkley Carver

I let the letter flutter to the floor and smirked over my shoulder. “Oh, I dare.”

My vision of Carver cocked his chin like he knew something, turned on his heel, and let himself out.

I grabbed the vines and swung as hard as I could. “I dare indeed.”

THE CITY OF DREAMS

IT WAS NEARING 10:00 PM so I ordered champagne. Not because I had a taste for it so much as it was the first extravagant beverage that came to mind.

I went out for some ice when my phone rang. The number started with 336, a North Carolina area code, a collection agency hotspot. My student loans hung over me like the Sword of Damocles. I sent the call to voicemail.

Okay back to work, I tapped my screen, opened the memo application and spoke into the microphone.

"What if there's something in the paint that turned the fantasy rooms into gateways to other dimensions?"

As I walked down the hall I couldn't help but notice the lack of room service trays, DO NOT DISTURB signs, and lights beneath the doors.

"What if an aspiring artist discovers a cellar filled with summoning substances: eye of newt, toe of frog, all bottled up and catalogued? What if he mixes them into his paints and his career takes off? He lands a gig painting the Oralia hotel where he leaves a little magic in each of the fantasy suites."

I paused and all I heard was the gentle hum of the lamps.

Either the mattresses weren't a-creaking or they were made from space aged memory foam.

"The problem is the artist is so confident he doesn't bother to draft a contract and the hotel shortchanges him. Destitute, he puts a curse on the 19th floor. The moral of the story: pay your freelancers."

I swished that idea around in my mouth and spat it out. "Too obvious."

The ice dispenser was at the far end of the hall, next to a row of vending machines. There were chips, soft drinks, and condoms. I'd never seen a condom dispenser so big that it sat on the floor, which was weird considering the limited selection. Sure, some items were ribbed and others were flavored, but nothing vibrated or glowed in the dark. Weirder still the coin slots, latches, and locks were covered in dust.

Each condom cost 75 cents, which was exactly what my curiosity was worth. I chose one with a horny little Devil logo.

I plucked the wrapper from the dispenser and flipped it over. The condom had expired. It hadn't been mating season in the fantasy suites for some time.

I hoped this wasn't an omen for my novel, or worse my career. I took the bucket back to the room with no clue what my story was going to be about. Whoever my characters were, whatever their situation was, they didn't feel like telling me about it tonight. Or had they?

When I got back I found the door was ajar.

Maybe someone else was on this floor.

I lifted the pale and prepared to give the ice bucket challenge to anyone I found skulking around. I cocked my cat-slipper back and kicked the door open.

It was Stephen, the bellhop. He leapt back. He cradled something to his chest as he caught his breath: a green bottle wrapped in golden foil. "Room service?"

I set the ice bucket on the kitchen counter and emptied the contents of my pullover.

He gave me a quizzical look. I followed his gaze to the condom in my left hand then to the phone in my right. He did the math. "So that's who you were talking to."

I feigned confusion. "Condoms don't talk."

He gave that an awkward nod and pointed his thumb over his shoulder. "Sorry, the door was open."

I nodded, wanting to say something, but finding myself consumed by the same brain fart afflicting him. He was cute when he was nervous.

"Well, you've got your champagne. Call me, I mean... call the front desk if you need anything, like a menu, or-I can bring you a menu in the morning."

"Please do."

And with that he recused himself.

I raised my phone. "What if the bellhop seduces his way into the guests' rooms, spikes their drinks, and harvests their organs?"

I looked out the peephole, kind of hoping to catch him looking back but he was gone.

•••

That night I awoke to crickets chirping, owls hooting, and birds singing in the distance. Water flowed down a babbling brook. A breeze rustled the reeds and shook the trees. I lay there, with my eyes shut, too afraid to move.

I smelled flowers in the air.

Something wet ran beneath my bicep, down my forearm, and into my palm. Even my neck felt slippery.

A coyote howled.

I shot up.

The moon was right there to greet me. I didn't start

breathing until I saw the cord sticking out of the lantern, and felt the mattress beneath my palms. I rolled around to find I had kicked the covers off, spilled champagne on the sheet, and drenched the pillow in sweat.

I leaned over the bed to pick the comforter off the floor and wrapped my arms around it like a long-lost friend.

I was in the Oralia, yet the crickets from my dream were still chirping.

The TV was on. A grove of evergreens swayed on screen. The northern lights filled the spaces between the branches, like neon curtains fluttering in the sky.

I fumbled around the nightstand for the remote. My forearm hit something heavy, knocking it over.

"Shit!" I yelled, thinking I'd hit a potted plant.

I checked the carpet and saw a power cord where I expected a trail of dirt. It turned out the big brass desk lamp was shaped like a bouquet of orchids. When I checked the TV I found the volume had turned up on its own. I pressed the GUIDE button to see the station was called RELAXING NIGHT FOREST SOUNDS. I pressed POWER and unplugged the TV.

•••

I realized it would be a while before I fell asleep, so I walked out onto the balcony. The table on the terrace was a slab of redwood atop a pair of moose antlers. The rustic furnishing had no effect on the surroundings. I set my champagne down, slouched into a chair, and scanned the horizon.

Looking down from the Oralia, Los Angeles was an endless grove of glass, logos, and light. There was a black splotch on the Hollywood Hills. A brush fire had left a trail of destruction all the way up to the Hollywood sign. The evergreens that lined the peak were still smoldering. The smoke had blotted out the moon. Take that, nature.

A breeze blew my hair into my face, leaving a strand of silver in my sightline. I'd changed color since I got here, so had the city. Those warm tungsten lamps, that lit so many romantic street scenes, had been replaced with cold LEDs, and the city of dreams felt more like a bad hallucination.

I reached into my pullover and raised my phone to my lips. "What if the story is about a girl who comes to tinsel town with dreams of making it as a screenwriter? She's naïve. She still thinks film is a transformative medium with the power to make other young women feel like they're not alone."

I took a swig of champagne, rolled the velvet taste around my pallet, and basked in the bubbles.

"What if she comes to Hollywood right as the independent studios shut down, and the big five studios set their sights on known brands. A time when fresh ideas take a back seat to nostalgia, and all filmmakers want to do is market men their childhood action figures back to them?"

I finished the glass in three long gulps. "What if hydrofrackers set up shop in her old back yard, her childhood home falls into sinkhole, and they refuse to take responsibility because it's in earthquake country? What if her mother's settlement barely affords her a trailer on the ass end of Reno, and now our hero has nowhere to go?"

I refilled the glass. "What if she finds herself selling romance novels in retail hell? What if her boyfriend discovers Polyamory in the middle of their relationship and only bothers to tell her when he gets caught? What if her mother's advice is: move to Silicon Valley and marry a startup company?"

I propped my chin in my hand. "What if our hero writes ghost stories not because she believes in the supernatural, but because she has problems letting go? What if by the time she makes that connection she's already mourning the life she's left behind?"

I cradled my head in my hands as the phone recorded my breathing.

A producer once asked if my screenplay was really about me. When I said, "Yes," he rolled a zippo down his knuckles, like a poker chip. He couldn't be bothered to feign interest. I don't remember what the pitch was, but I remember that his lighter had a Sigil of Baphomet on it. No matter how energized I got I couldn't draw his eyes away from that goat-faced engraving. There was an inscription on the bottom, but I couldn't quite make it out.

I was surprised he had any notes at the end, but he told me I put too much of myself into the script, which hurt it, because I wasn't very likeable.

He added that the real tragedy was that in this climate of female empowerment my script might actually get made.

That shit stuck.

I tapped the memo app off and slid it into my pullover. I took a deep breath, raised my palms up, exhaled, and lowered them.

There was a terrible buzzing behind me, like a bee trapped inside a megaphone. I turned around to find a drone, a little quadcopter with a camera, hovering over the railing.

"No shit."

The drone ascended and circled my head, attempting to see if I was someone whose tears were worth recording.

I gave the lens a "one moment" gesture, opened the sliding door, and stepped into the parlor. Hidden from the camera's sightline I put some things into position, leaned out, and beckoned the drone in.

The swing was positioned right in front of the balcony, ideal for exhibitionists who enjoyed scenic sex or writers who wanted to use it as a slingshot. I launched my ice bucket at the drone, knocked out its propellers, and sent it swirling down.

I wasn't a likeable character, but I'd be damned if I wasn't resourceful.

• • •

I awoke to a low rumble, followed by a concussive boom. Leaves fell on my face. This time I didn't panic.

Growing up on a fault line I'd gotten used to Richter scale wake up calls. My earliest memory was of my mother catching plates, snatching me up, and dragging me beneath the doorframe.

I took a deep breath and mentally prepared myself to roll out of bed and crawl for the closet. I tried to sit up, but I was pinned down. I expected to feel the weight of one of those prop branches on my chest instead I felt nothing below my collar.

The source of the rumbling shifted in my mind, from the earth quaking to thunder clapping. There was a flash. My eyes opened to thick droplets of rain bursting on my forehead.

I was lying in the middle of an old growth forest, soaking in a stew of wood chips and twigs. Floodwater splashed against my thighs and puddled around the trees, trees I'd recognized from an old National Geographic foldout. I'd read they grew taller than the Statue of Liberty and thick enough to drive trucks through. Their branches creaked like old rocking chairs and their leaves spiraled all around me.

I was paralyzed. I told myself this had to be a dream. My mind had stitched this landscape together from snapshots of Redwood National Park, Kings Canyon, and Yosemite. Now I was going on a little trip through my subconscious.

I tried to turn my head, wiggle my toes, and make a fist, all the things I'd read to do when sleep paralysis had a hold of you, but nothing worked.

Lightning flickered. A shadow leapt across the canopy. It had curled horns, a pointed beard, broad shoulders, and long furry legs. Thunder crashed when it landed.

The shadow's hooves splashed through the rainwater. Its glowing red eyes drew a line in the dark as it sidestepped around me.

I kept trying to make appeals to my intellect.

I thought: *The Devil is just a faun gone wrong. Greeks believed fauns helped weary travelers find their way through the forest. They weren't demons. They were the dolphins of the mainland.*

But the closer this faun got the more obvious it became he wasn't there to help. He was a mammoth with biceps as thick as car axels, fingers as thick as rolling pins, and nails as long as daggers. His legs were less like those of a goat and more like those of a camel with long matted wool, and his hooves were larger than any horses' I'd ever seen.

This faun wouldn't lead me anywhere I wanted to go. He circled, flared his nostrils, and exhaled smoke.

I told myself *Theologians demonized fauns because the Greeks kept making idols of them and their giant dongs. Before the Satanic makeover fauns were just neighborly nudists.*

The shadow knelt over me, reached down and grabbed me by the temples. Had he wanted to he could have crushed my skull like a tomato.

I sent a series of signals to my limbs hoping one would take. *Make a fist. Bend your knee. Turn your feet.* I started to feel movement in my big toe, but by then it was too late.

The shadow pressed his cheek to mine. His flesh was caked in ash and coal, and he stunk of soot, like he'd just crawled out of an industrial chimney.

He licked my earlobe with his forked tongue.

"I can smell your soul... Soon I will taste it."

I wiggled my big toe as hard as I could until I willed myself to kick.

I rolled out of bed onto the floor and ran out of the room into the parlor. Not seeing where I was going I charged straight into the sex swing.

I swung forward and fell back on the floor. There were no demons behind me, no trees or falling leaves, only a strange and lonely room. I lay there as the cold reality of the hotel settled back in.

• • •

I paced between the 19th floor and the 18th floor, strangling the railing with one hand and my phone with the other.

Matilda MacDonald was on the other end. “No, you cannot telecommute.”

There was a rustling. Matilda was talking to someone with her thumb over the receiver.

I rolled my eyes at someone who couldn’t see me. “He’s there, isn’t he? Just put him on.”

The rustling returned.

“You saw something. Didn’t you?” Barkley said, joining the conversation.

“I had a bad dream. I think this place is more distracting than it is inspiring.

“It puts you on edge, doesn’t it? Good. Use it.”

“If you’re just looking for a sense of atmosphere I can take some photos of the room and review them from home.”

Barkley breathed into the receiver. I imagined him taking off his aviators in a show of sympathy.

“I’ll tell you what. Matilda has been staring at microfiche all night, sifting through the Oralia’s records to give you some back story, and you know what she’s found?”

“Print has been dead for a long time?”

"There have been no murders, no suicides, nothing of note in that room. What you and I encountered may have shaken us to our cores, but its bark is worse than its bite."

"What about the people who built this place? Why did they make a theme park of haunted hotel clichés?"

"You just answered your own question. Tourism."

"Yeah, but what about the owner?"

"I'd love to tell you there's a H.H. Holmes figure crawling through secret passages and murdering guests, but the hotel is owned by a series shell corporations."

I felt my neck. My pulse was still racing. *Stimulate the anterior insula and you too can see a ghost.* "Do you mind if I ask you something about the night you saw the demon?"

"You want to know if I was fighting with my wife?"

"I was going to ask if you were under a lot of stress."

"Oh yeah, I was. Mona did not care for the suite. Not one bit. She said if I wanted to fuck her in a forest we should've gone camping.'"

I paced the landing as the gears turned in my mind. "There is something off about the room, nothing paranormal, but I think if I have to have nightmares I'd rather have them at home."

Barkley made a clicking sound with his tongue. "I'm certain there's something there. Healthy people don't see things at the first sign of strain."

I pinched the bridge of my nose. "Healthy people see things all the time. Where do you think all those reports of angels, aliens, and shadow people come from?"

"Shadow people?"

"Google it."

Everything in the Oralia was nightmare fuel: the art deco entrance, the gargoyles on the way in, the mirrored lift, all of it.

I looked toward the door to the 19th floor, waiting for the

irrational fear to pass. "Can you tell me anything about the hotel, anything at all?"

I heard Carver riffling through his pages. "There are no burial mounds in the basement if that's what you're asking."

"Nothing?"

"No guests floating in the water tank. No chutes for disposing bodies. Nothing."

"In other words. No cause for alarm."

"Nope. None. No real reason not to go back up there and earn that advance."

"Okay." I rubbed my forehead. "You do know that's not how advances work, right?"

But the line was dead before I could get a response.

THE MAP IS NOT THE TERRAIN

THIS IS how classy the Oralia's continental breakfast was, there were no cantaloupe slices, no stale doughnuts, and no towers of off brand cereals. It was all eggs benedict, frittatas, and quiches as far as the eye could see. I filled a thermos and badgered as much food as I could carry.

Stephen spotted me on my way up.

"Do you need help with that?"

I was balancing a stack of Styrofoam containers beneath my chin. "That seems like a good idea." I said, relieved to have another set of hands.

Stephen led the way into the mirrored elevator.

This time he had no qualms with looking at my reflection. "Sleep well last night?"

I flashed a smile. "No, I saw a demon."

Stephen's reaction was delayed. He lowered an eyebrow. "You're being facetious, right?"

I gave him a so-so gesture. "It was nightmare, but my benefactor says it's the reason why I'm here."

Stephen didn't seem surprised. He knew more about my

arrangement with Barkley then he'd led on. "Do you want me to charge some ghost hunting gear to the room?"

I nodded. "Not because I need it. Just to freak out my benefactor."

"I could get you one of those recorders. You could try talking to the demon. See it says anything."

"Electronic voice phenomenon?"

Stephen tilted his neck with a bit of swagger. "EVP, yeah you know me."

"You know how that works, right? The recorder just raises the volume when things get quiet. You end up having a conversation with your own heartbeat."

Stephen feigned a serious nod of consideration. "So yes then?"

"Oh for sure."

"Do you need an EMF meter as well?"

"Yes and a spirit box."

"Maybe a night vision camera?"

"Yes and a Ouija board."

"A deck of Tarot Cards?"

"Yes and a magic 8-ball."

I suddenly felt very safe staying in this hotel. "Perhaps you should be writing this stuff down."

We spent the rest of the ride smiling at each other's reflections.

•••

Back on my floor I set the breakfast buffet on the floor outside my suite. I spread Barkley's outline across the carpet, all ten double-spaced pages of it. I opened my memo pad, rolled up my sleeves, and guzzled some coffee.

I sat there in the lotus position trying my best to summon a story out of what lay before me.

A vision of Barkley came to me instead. He took his time too, wandering out of the elevator like he wasn't sure where I'd be. I waved, not that surprised to see him.

"Barkley."

"Noelle."

He was in a full captain's uniform. His eyes hid beneath a cap with golden laurels on the bill, his chest was lined with medals that swayed back and forth, and his blazer was fastened with brass buttons that clinked as he walked.

Barkley bent over and circled his outline; he touched down on page one and started reading. "Hunter Crenshaw is a trucker whose life is swirling in the shitter."

I wrote as I spoke, "Is Barkley married to the name Hunter?"

Barkley took a toy 747 from his pocket and glided it over the page. "Hunter is careening down the Highway, with a rig filled with 4k HDR Ultravision Home Theater Systems, when he passes out. He wakes up to find he's wearing a bag of Carnitos, a melted Belmont Bar, and a can of Canyon Brew. Worse still, his rig has crashed into a motel. Lucky for Hunter the building is covered in overgrowth."

I raised an eyebrow. "Why are you peppering the story with all these brand names?"

Barkley tilted his head back and forth. "It gives it a greater sense of authenticity."

I rubbed my forehead. "Jesus, Barkley, you're the Michael Bay of literature."

Barkley brushed that notion off.

"Hunter finds a flashlight in his glove box, stumbles into the motel, and scares a family of possums. He presses on to find the inn is filled with fantasy rooms, *dark* fantasy rooms. He finds a BDSM dungeon with barred windows, shackles, and chains. He wanders through a ballroom with masked statues, a chandelier on the floor, and a set of wooden stocks. His path leads to a room dressed like Stonehenge. There's a mural of the countryside, artificial turf, and Styrofoam stones."

Barkley waved his 747 over the next page.

"Hunter raids the mini fridge and discovers a bottle of Crown Empire Vodka. He polishes it off and crashes on the room's Cloud 9 Memory Foam Mattress."

I scribbled some notes. "Not sure if those brands want to be associated with that environment, but whatever."

Barkley stepped behind me, knelt down, and leaned over my shoulder. He smelt of Aqua Velva and menthol. "Hunter wakes up chained to a slab surrounded by cloaked druids, all chanting like Gregorian monks."

"Those religious orders definitely don't go together."

Barkley clawed at the air. "The Devil crawls forth from the shadows and circles the slab. He's got wild burning eyes and drool running down his muzzle. He straddles our hero. Hunter begs for his life. The Devil offers to spare him if, and only if, Hunter can provide six souls for the price of one."

Barkley raised his pilot's cap. His eyes widened. "Desperate, Hunter stalks the surrounding campgrounds, scours the roads for hitchhikers, and lies in wait in rest stops. He abducts a young woman and brings her back to the motel as an offering."

I made a timeout gesture. "What if she stole a large deposit from her office? Let's say she checks into the motel thinking Hunter is the owner. Maybe she overhears him arguing with... I want to say, his mother. Perhaps something terrible could happen to her in the shower?"

The reference went over Barkley's head. "No fluff. Keep it simple."

Barkley was notorious for giving his serial killers more pages than his protagonists. In this synopsis everything was streamlined, there was no detective to slow Hunter down, and no pesky backstories to humanize the victims. They were just meat at the end of Hunter's knife. Why should they have nice lives?

The rest of Barkley's notes read like torture porn. He acted out each explicit detail. He pantomimed pouring chloroform, holding a victim in his arms, and slamming a trunk. He pulled the air by the hair, shackled his victim, and stretched duct tape across her mouth. He picked the top buttons off her blouse, one by one. Then he ripped it open. He gripped a phantom throat and flicked his wrist back and forth, as though he were slitting it.

Barkley was having too much fun exploring the space to notice the look on my face.

I folded the last page into an airplane and flung it down the hall. "I could've totally telecommuted for this."

My vision of Barkley made a so-so gesture. "I wanted you to see the lay of the land before you started construction."

I gathered the pages without much care for their order. "Now I see I'm building a house on sand."

I could tell Barkley was forming a rebuttal, but I went into the suite and slammed the door on him.

•••

I looked out over the balcony and the mountains were gone. I tried to find the Hollywood sign, but the hills had faded as well. Even the skyscrapers were lost in the smog.

There was a smoke advisory in effect. Still this was the only way I could see daylight without revoking my contract.

After watching Barkley's interpretive dance, I spent the rest of the morning researching sleep disorders. I'd found a person with a history of depression was more likely to experience paralysis, add social anxiety to the mix and they were more likely to sense a presence (visit the sleep paralysis project's website if you want to retrace my steps). Depression, anxiety, and problems sleeping have all been linked to low serotonin. Our brains are primed to produce serotonin when we see the sun, so I was out on the ledge getting my treatment.

I looked back into the smog and raised my collar over my mouth like a surgical mask. I'd worry about the air once I started coughing until then I planned to work on my tan.

I leaned over the railing. A sheet of smog covered the ground. The Oralia looked like it was floating in the clouds. The surrounding buildings looked like the spires of heaven.

It was surreal, especially since my research had moved onto the gospels. The volume on hand was no Gideon bible. It was bound in wood, it had silver hinges, and an engraving stating it was made exclusively for the room.

I was sifting through the text for signs of Satan.

In pop culture the Devil had devolved into a genie with a bad user agreement. He granted wishes, but terms and conditions always applied. He'd throw out a disclaimer about free will, but the ultimate moral was never that cerebral, it was always: material rewards are never as valuable as those of the soul.

Barkley's story tweaked that formula by removing the morality play. His Devil threatens Hunter Crenshaw into doing his bidding for the sake of survival. Hunter stalks and murders innocents, but he isn't choosing to do so on his own. He's a slasher with a powerful benefactor.

I didn't care much for Satan as a predatory lender or as the voice on a serial killer's shoulder. So I decided to go back to the source material to find the definitive Devil.

The problem was the Devil had too many names: *Abaddon, Apollyon, Antichrist, Beelzebub, Belial, Diabolos, Leviathan, Lucifer, Legion,* Mephistopheles, *and Satan.*

The Lord of the Flies, the Chief of the Demons, the arch fiend. The great red dragon, the serpent, the roaring lion, the beast. The god of this world, the unholy spirit, the wicked one.

The King of Babylon and the bottomless pit. The Father of Lies and the Son of Perdition. The Lightbringer and the Prince of Darkness. The morning star and the ruler of the night.

The destroyer, the deceiver, the slanderer, the adversary, the accuser, the tempter, the butcher, the baker, and the candlestick maker. The list went on and on.

Paging through the scriptures, I couldn't help but wonder: *Did theologians reduce a whole host of demons into the Devil for the sake of branding?*

One description made the Devil out to be a high-ranking cherub. From what I could tell the Cherubim were the lookers of the angels, muscular giants, bejeweled in precious stones.

Ezekiel spent several verses describing their fashion sense. The Cherubim were nothing like something you'd find in a Victoria's Secret catalogue. They didn't have sexy little wings. They had four broad ones. Each wingtip had a fully functional hand and every feather was covered in eyeballs.

Unlike Cupid, each cherub had four faces: an eagle, a lion, a bull, and a man. What made them even more haunting were the four wheels that floated around them like psychic gyroscopes. Oh and every inch of their wheels and bodies...also covered in eyeballs.

Like the Minotaur, centaurs, and, griffins, the cherubim seemed like a combo platter of random limbs. The Devil started as this class of angel but at some point, artists decided he ought to look like a faun, a smaller combination of limbs, but a human animal hybrid all the same. I figured this was because fauns were horny and the church was chaste so they decided to put horns on the Devil's face.

I tapped the memo button on my phone. "I'm not sure about Barkley, but a gyroscopic eyeball monster would've freaked me out so much more."

The sliding door opened behind me, I turned to find my

imaginary vision of Barkley Carver stepping out onto the balcony.

"So now you can just come and go as you please?" I asked.

Barkley set his captains cap on the table. "I've been listening in. You're dumping lots of exposition into your narration. I'm here to help work it into a conversation."

"Uh, okay." I signaled to the open chair with a nervous smile. I'd slammed the door in his face a few hours ago. Here he was again. I wondered if he'd leave if I asked him to. Barkley took the seat, put his boots up on the redwood slab, and interlocked his fingers behind his head. "Why waste time researching the Devil when he's a brand everyone knows?"

I lowered my shirt from my mouth. "Because his brand has gotten stale. Horror cracks over time, what scared people a generation ago won't work on millennials."

Barkley unbuttoned his blazer. "Have you found something better?"

I made a so-so gesture, scrolled through some articles on my phone, and raised a finger at one I'd bookmarked. "Did you know one of the first heretics thought the Old Testament God, with all his jealousy and wrath, was the Devil in disguise?"

Barkley undid his cufflinks. "Let's not put that in there. Questioning the gospels is a long way from keeping things simple."

I shrugged. "I'm just trying to approach the Devil from an interesting angle."

Barkley reached into his blazer, flipped his aviator shades open, and put them on. "What else do you got?"

I flicked through an image gallery on my phone. "John's description of the beast in Revelations could be something worth exploring. It had seven heads, ten horns, ten matching crowns, lions' teeth, the posture of a leopard, and the feet of a bear."

Barkley waved his fingers. "I'd love to see that fight Godzilla but I don't think it'll fit into a motel setting."

I kept swiping. "There's an illustration in the *Codex Gigas* we could play with."

Barkley snapped his fingers to jog his memory. "The so-called Devil's Bible?"

I nodded as I read. "Unearthed in Bohemia in the early 12th century."

"Let's see it."

I showed Barkley the fabled illustration. The Codex featured a horned Devil with a reptilian face, red lips, twin tongues, big hands, and feet equipped with Velociraptor talons.

Barkley lowered his shades. "He looks like he's wearing a snakeskin swim cap and a lizard-skin diaper."

I looked at it again. Carver wasn't wrong.

Barkley pushed his shades back up. "Do you have anything better than horns, hooves, and a tail? Anything more chilling than a goat walking among the living tempting them to sin?"

I set my phone on the table and gave it a spin. "A lot of that is Dante and Milton's fan fiction."

"Yes, but right now that's the Devil people know."

I rolled my eyes toward the smog on the skyline, to the golden city of angels in the clouds.

There was a buzzing below the balcony. A drone rose through the smog. It was another quadcopter, hoping to catch celebrities hooking up in their natural habitat. Its lens zoomed in to where I sat. I waved. The pilot must've recognized me, because the drone flew back into the smog from whence it came.

I turned and Barkley was gone.

A HILL WORTH DYING ON

MATILDA HAD SUMMONED me to the cocktail longue. She started with small talk and pleasantries until she was two drinks in, and then the red in her face started showing. She tilted her chin, furrowed her brow, and shook her head. "You threw out Barkley's entire outline."

I put my hands up. "Not true. I used the whole thing."

The bartender brought Matilda another whiskey.

She took a sip and said, "You broke the cardinal rule of writing" she chopped at the table to emphasize each word, "Do-not-make-yourself-the-hero."

I flattened my palms on the counter, ready to hold my ground. "I thought the cardinal rule of writing is: write what you know."

Matilda threw her hands up. "When someone hires you to ghostwrite a story, you don't make the hero a ghostwriter."

I finished my drink and wondered if this was the hill I wanted to die on? "Barkley put me up here because he wanted me to capture the authentic experience. It just rings truer from my point of view."

Matilda raised a perfectly plucked eyebrow. "When I said

Barkley wanted to try something new I didn't mean he wanted to throw the baby out with bathwater. I meant he wanted to dabble in the paranormal without sacrificing his trademarks. You have to have a serial killer, a heap of bodies, and yes, a bunch of product tie-ins to supplement all of our incomes." Matilda pointed her thumb to herself and her index finger to me.

I shrugged. "Technically his trademarks, and all the tie-ins, are still here."

Matilda flipped to a page that was nothing but red lines all the way down. "Ah yes, when you talked to a projection of Barkley, like you're Russell Crowe in *A Beautiful Mind.* The captain's uniform was a nice touch, but the whole fantasy prone personality thing... Your hyperbolic process from the podcast... I ran it by one of Barkley's consultants. He says the psychiatric community is still debating if such a thing exists. So are you bonkers or just an unreliable narrator?"

"A little of column A, a little of column B. But never mind all that Matilda just try to follow me here, how do you make buyers out of a generation of cynics? You make fun of your product placement. It's backhanded. It's ironic, but nevertheless it builds brand awareness."

Matilda waved that line of reasoning away. "Carver once devoted an entire chapter to the sleek design, roomy interior, and smooth handling of the Pegasus Prestige. His readers don't care."

I rubbed my forehead. "I would."

"Worry about his readers." She tapped the draft in her lap. "I shouldn't tell you that Barkley liked what I read him. He's even open to having a female lead. Lord knows his books could use one. The problem is *this,*" she slapped the manuscript, "doesn't sound like him."

"You could say he's entering a new phase." Matilda shook her head. "Barkley doesn't describe locations unless they're crime scenes. So the Oralia has a mirrored elevator? So do a lot of hotels. There's no sense mentioning it unless you plan on using it."

"It adds ambience."

"Cut it."

I hid behind my empty glass. "If Barkley wanted more of the same he would've stuck with his writing pool."

Matilda downed the rest of her whiskey, creaked her neck, and sighed. "You know Ann M. Martin wrote 35 *Baby-Sitters Club* books. 35. That's more titles than Sylvia Plath, Harper Lee, or J. D. Salinger combined. Yet young readers wanted more than she could deliver. Is Martin any less of an artist because she worked with ghostwriters?"

Matilda's math didn't add up.

"Harper Lee labored over of *To Kill a Mockingbird* for over-"

Matilda waved her hand through my argument before it could even form.

"This isn't just about money for Barkley either. He wants you to be part of something. He picked you because he thinks you have what it takes to share in his legacy. That's a big deal. You should take it seriously."

"I do." I spoke to Matilda's reflection across the bar. "I just want this story to be something I would want to read."

"I get that, I really do, but you have to make it more his than yours," Matilda looked to my reflection "because frankly Noelle you're not a very likeable character."

Matilda settled her tab, straightened her coat, and passed off the marked-up manuscript. "You have three weeks to turn this thing around."

•••

I stepped into the elevator, tapped the button for the 19th

floor, and did my best to avoid eye contact with myself. The infinite mirror effect unnerved me.

I was always baffled by my own reflection, with my sharp cheekbones and little dashes for nostrils. How was that a face? It was no less strange when there was a mile of them staring at me from here into forever. All those wide offset eyes were haunting. Not as scary as having just three weeks to write an entire novel. Matilda might as well have asked me to spin straw into gold.

I focused on the corner, to avoid my reflections, and raised my phone. "What if the main character wasn't an author anymore? What if she walks away from creative endeavors and becomes a copywriter?"

I looked back to find my reflections nodding at this notion.

"What if she takes her mother's advice, heads out to Silicon Valley, and starts gold-digging?"

My reflections shrugged in unison.

"What if she builds her life around home care and children? Could she exhaust her artistic ambitions with adult coloring books, jewelry, and crocheting? Could she substitute her love of fiction with book club selections? Would she live happily ever after? Is there such a thing?"

My reflections raised their collective eyebrows. We were skeptical. The elevator dinged and split my smirk in half.

I spun around to bid the rest of my reflections adieu. "Good chat ladies. I'll try to come up with some reason for your inclusion later."

THE BLACK DOOR

I SAT cross-legged on the crooked redwood slab out on the balcony, listening to the city speak. Drivers laid on their horns, revved their engines, and screeched through intersections. So many sirens whaled at once the streets sounded like they were weeping. There was a domestic dispute a few floors down. I couldn't tell what the couple was arguing about, but judging by their tone one of them was due to fly over the railing at any moment.

I blamed the full moon for everything: the chaos, the noise, Matilda. The moon loomed on the horizon, looking closer to the earth than it possibly could've been, a bowling ball about to roll over the buildings like they were pins.

I was convinced the moon had an impact on human behavior, even if all research on the "Lunar effect" had yet to produce a shred of evidence. The gravitational pull was doing something. That big yellow rock was driving Los Angeles insane.

I drew a long breath. The air was thick with the stench of desperation.

They say in LA you're never more than 50 feet away from a

screenplay. There's always another hack writer willing to strike a Faustian bargain to stave off eviction. Now I was one of them. I sold my soul just to get the creditors off my voicemail.

I wondered what doors Barkley's influence would open. Maybe my next gig would have me writing punch up notes for a movie based on a toy line, or a cartoon based on a mobile game, or, what the hell, an adaptation of a popular ad campaign into a feature film.

I was lucky to get this opportunity. So what if that meant shoehorning product placement into my writing? It wasn't my name I'd be smearing. Barkley Carver had enough shame to go around.

Still, I didn't want to go back inside. The room was haunted by my humiliation. So I sat out there soaking in the commotion. Seagulls squawked. A plane flew low overhead. A sliding door slammed a few floors down and I started to cry.

A familiar buzz arose from bellow the balcony. I peered over the railing to find another drone approaching. The quad-copter ascended, spun around, and zoomed in on me.

I flashed a peace sign, before it occurred to me to wipe my cheeks down. The damn drone had caught me crying again. It was embarrassing, but I made no motion toward the sex-swing I'd used to shoot the last one down. I was a nobody. My tears would never net a profit for anyone, and so I sat.

The drone flew over the railing, across the table, and hummed in my face.

I smiled. "Well, you're a brave one aren't you?"

I looked into the lens like the eye of a sympathetic friend.

"Do you ever feel like this city is slowly digesting your soul?"

I'm not sure if the drone had a microphone, but it bobbed up and down like it understood.

•••

I was pacing the 19th floor at three in the morning. I was more than a little tipsy. To make matters worse, the light fixtures had started flickering. This hall was where I did the bulk of my thinking, writing, and verbal processing since I'd checked in. Something had to be done.

I decided to place a call to the front desk. I dug my phone out of my pullover. The voice memo application was still running from God knows when. A little waveform trailed across the screen. In the upper right corner I saw that my battery was at 10%.

Then the screen blinked off, and I heard a screech, like someone pushing furniture across a hardwood floor, followed by a crash and a door creaking open.

I checked the rooms. The suites with the vampire bat knocker, the wolf, the octopus, and mine were all shut.

A dozen ice cubes scattered across the floor. The icemaker tilted forward and spat out another mouthful of blocks and fell on its face. The condom dispenser, behind it, stood diagonal from the wall. There was a tall black door where the dispenser had been. The top of the door was adorned with a carving of three figures, holding hands, pointing downward.

What kind of hotel puts a condom dispenser in front of a door? The Oralia, of course.

I approached with caution. By the time I stepped onto the tiles the ice cubes had started melting. Water seeped into my cat slippers while I was busy examining the scene.

This new door had a knocker in the same place as the others. It featured a figure sitting atop the big brass ring with his fist to his chin. It took a moment to recognize Rodin's famous sculpture *The Thinker*.

I moved closer and the other engravings revealed themselves as well. At first I thought they were simple floral designs, until I shifted my footing and a glare caught the finish —naked figures jumped out of the woodwork, twisted, writhing, and anguished, a collage of biceps, buttocks, and breasts. Each carving looked like it had melted into position, a liquid orgy of delight and despair.

The lights flickered and the figures seemed to crawl over each other. I jumped back and they vanished back into the varnish. I was too tipsy to trust what I was seeing.

I squeezed my eyes shut, raised my palms, and inhaled; I lowered my palms, exhaled, and opened my eyes. *The Thinker* watched me from the knocker waiting for me to make my move.

My curiosity got the better of me. I took the ring and knocked three times. Each hit echoed into the distance. When the last fell silent the door opened.

I stepped through the entryway to find not carpeting but cold stones. I felt the wall for a light switch and found more stones. I dared to announce my presence. “Hello?”

The door swung shut behind me and there was a clicking not far from where I stood.

I froze a few steps from the archway. Behind me was only darkness. Ahead was the crackling of a flame drawing me into the room. I followed the light toward the bedroom, taking in my surroundings as I went. The furnishings were made up of inquisition era torture devices: Catherine wheels, Judas Cradles, and Iron Maidens. Cat o’ nine tails, riding crops, and stocks were scattered on the floor while the walls were lined with shackles.

Something about that flame beckoned me. I followed the light to a pair of torches mounted to an archway. Standing at the threshold a breeze hit me harder than anything I expected from any bedroom.

I stepped through the archway and entered a cathedral so grand there was no way it fit inside the city, let alone the 19th floor of the Oralia. Torches ran from the floor to the dome of the ceiling. Firelights went so far off into the distance they seemed like constellations.

Each torch sat in the eye socket of a slick red skull. The skulls were stacked higher than any catacomb, and held together with a mortar of musculature and organs.

Support beams marked each of the columns. They looked like thighbones, with curved bodies and rounded joints, but they were longer than anything on the fossil record, longer than canoes, longer than limousines.

The vestibule was a cobblestone platform the size of a tennis court. Beyond that were steps so wide and so deep they could've been coliseum seats. They led to a swirling volcanic cauldron at the heart of the cathedral.

Tall flowing banners hung from the walls. Light danced down their fabric revealing a patchwork of hair, veins, and nipples. The banners were made from human flesh, flesh that had been branded with a ghastly coat of arms. I couldn't help but examine the nearest banner. There was a rendering of Adam and Eve, naked as the day they were made, shackled to a shield, topped with a crown of horns, framed with raven wings. Upon the shield were the beasts of the sea and the dragon of the earth as described in Revelations.

The worst part of the cathedral was the cages hanging from the ceiling like a colony of bats, some were filled with people I'd known: producers I'd pitched to, agents I'd tried to court, and screenwriters who'd vanished.

I inched toward the stairway that went around the cathedral. Something was happening at the bottom. Lava shot up like a glowing orange geyser and all the cages rattled.

There was a pulsing hum, whoosh whoosh whoosh, followed by a series of sharp metallic clinks like an aircraft carrier haling up an anchor. Something terrible was swimming in that fire.

And then it emerged: a hulking titan with four giant batwings. At first I thought it was covered in boils, big white puss filled sacks, but then the boils squinted and I realized I was looking at eyeballs.

The titan's head was a lopsided jumble with the profiles of beasts in place of his ears. The fangs of a lion roared out of his left side, while the snout of a bull flared out from his right. The grimace facing forward was human, as human as a chiseled brick could get. I tried to read his face, but despite his size, the titan was so far away it was hard to make out his expression.

This was the entity Ezekiel described in the bible: a Seraph of the highest order of angels, one of the Cherubim corrupted by his fall. This was no mere Devil. This was Satan.

Something told me not to look him in the eyes so I shifted my gaze to the ceiling. The cages started rattling. The captives went into violent convulsions. Their backs stiffened, their legs jutted out, and their toes pointed straight down. The prisoners gripped their bars as electricity surged through them. They gritted their teeth until their eyes rolled back and their jaws went slack. Light burst from their eye-sockets, nostrils, and mouths.

The prisoners sat up in a uniform position. "COME CLOSER." They spoke as one, a congregation echoing a sermon.

"I can hear you just fine up here."

"CLOSER."

Thunder boomed. The floor quaked. The platform tilted downward. I looked for the archway, but it was high above me now. I could already feel a pull toward the cauldron. I fell back desperately trying to lower my center of gravity. I dug my heels into the gaps, but my slippers offered no traction and I lost my footing.

From the edge of the platform all the way to the pit, the steps fell like dominos. The coliseum transformed into a mile-long ramp. When the platform tilted I slid fast. The traction peeled my sweatpants up to my knees. The stones scraped my calves, chaffed my thighs, and battered my ass. They struck my tailbone, every column of my spine, and slammed into the back of my skull.

Satan's caged congregation followed my movements. I fell so fast their eyes passed like comets.

I looked down into the cauldron. Satan's wheels lowered into the lava, making it swirl and bubble. He waded in to meet me head on. *CLOSER*. When I neared the pit he opened wide to swallow me whole.

A FINE ART

I WOKE up hanging from the sex swing: my legs entangled in the vines, my back pressed into the polyester, my cheek raw with carpet burn, the fibers hardened by the drool running down my chin.

Wine hangovers are like corkscrews through your temples.

I rolled onto my back. The canopy spun, making it seem like clouds passing over the sun. The vents added to the illusion that I was lying in a prairie with a breeze caressing my skin.

I fumbled around my pockets until I realized my phone had found its way into my bra. The battery probably wasn't dead when I fell asleep, but it was now. It's hard for horror writers to isolate their victims when they can call for help with the push of a button. Figures my subconscious also had to kill the battery before scaring me.

Still dangling from the swing, I rolled over, crawled to the outlet, and plugged my phone in. I watched the screen with one eye open until it powered on. I tapped the memo application.

"Why would Satan eat me when the rest of his collection

was up in a showroom? Silly subconscious. Learn to follow your own internal log...ick."

Nausea turned in my stomach like a dog looking for a place to sit.

There was a knock on the door. "Housekeeping."

I tried to wriggle free but the swing had twisted around my legs.

Stephen entered the room pulling a vacuum cleaner. He wore the same uniform he always wore just with an apron. He made it all the way to the outlet before he spotted me dangling from the sex swing. He just smiled. "Need a hand?"

"If you're not busy?"

Stephen slowly untwisted the swing. "I take it somebody had fun last night?"

"I think so," I said, nearly tumbling to the floor. Stephen caught me in time to ease me to the carpet.

"Want to get a drink?"

Stephen grinned. "It's nine in the morning."

"It's cool. I'm an alcoholic."

I may have stroked his cheek before passing back out. I can't say with certainty, but I wouldn't put it past me.

•••

When I came to I found Stephen had left me a Gatorade on the counter with a post-it note that read DRINK ME. It settled my stomach, but my headache refused to wane, so I went down to the cafeteria in search of a cure. I ordered scrambled eggs, a glass of apple juice, with a huge side of ibuprofen. When I regained my balance, I went to the gift shop, bought a pocket printer, and returned to the room. On my laptop I opened so many tabs there was no room to display their titles, hit print, and watched the inkjet run out of colors.

When the cartridge was drained, I gathered a stack of pages and took them with me into the hall.

No one had confirmed my suspicion, but after a few weeks I figured I had the 19th floor to myself. So I paced the hall, stretched my legs, and dictated the dream into my phone. "I had a hunch I'd seen the door before. It was the knocker that gave it away."

The top page of my stack featured a close up of a contemplative figure, sitting on his stoop, ignoring the writhing bodies behind him.

"It was Rodin's *The Thinker*, a piece he shrunk and hid inside his sculpture *The Gates of Hell*."

I turned the page to find a white version of the big black door from my dream. The next page featured the three huddling figures facing downward.

"Originally, the figures on top weren't pointing to the door, but to the phrase *Abandon hope all ye who enter here*, something Rodin stole from Dante's Inferno, that I guess I'm stealing now...I think my subconscious painted the door black so it wouldn't have to represent each figure's dimensions all at once."

I flipped through my pages. Several casts had been made of Rodin's seminal sculpture in plaster and bronze. I found a close up of his depiction of *Dante's Inferno*: the writhing naked forms, layered upon each other like meats in a pie tin. None of the Oralia's knockers seemed all that menacing in comparison.

I came to a page with an etching of a cell filled with Judas cradles, stretch racks and a fresh victim dangling from a pulley system.

"My dream got the decor from a medieval torture chamber, while the Cathedral was stolen from H.R. Giger."

The next page featured the bar from the H.R. Giger Museum. The arches were built with vertebras. The vaulted ceiling was lined with ribs, and the support beams were wrapped in twisted spinal columns.

"If you're going to steal, steal from the best, right?"

The next page featured the etching on *The Devil* Tarot card. It reminded me of the coat of arms that had been scorched onto the banner in my dream. Demon versions of Adam and Eve stood naked chained to the Devil's perch.

I paged through a small gallery of illustrations of the Cherubim. None of the artists could come to a consensus on what these angels were supposed to look like. Some wore their wheels like gyroscopes, others like halos, and others let them trail behind them. Some wore their excess wings like cloaks, some like pants, and others had wings in place of limbs. The only thing the artists agreed on was that these creatures had four heads.

My subconscious must've stocked up on even more nightmare fuel while I was researching the Devil. It evolved Barkley's big black faun into a cosmic giant. Barkley's dream took him to the woods outside his childhood home. Mine took me into the dungeons of my memory palace. Leave it to my subconscious to try to one up the competition.

My second nightmare contradicted everything about the first and it did it without borrowing anything from the room. This dream had no use for giant redwoods, full moons, and rock faces. This didn't disprove Barkley's theory that the suite was haunted. It merely reinforced my theory that dreams can be more powerful than we realize.

Still the Oralia had lost some of its mystique. It was as Barkley implied a quirky Hollywood theme park to draw in tourists. The air of menace had vented. It felt safe to get back to work. I just had to take a quick peek behind the condom dispenser to be sure.

I held my phone up, like a talisman to ward off evil. I let my superstition do the walking while my intellect did the talking. "Dreams have long been interpreted as prophecy. John of Patmos took his nightmares as visions of the end times. Dream logic is strangely compelling, fostering a feeling that bypasses empirical evidence. Even to folks who hear about it after the fact. It's probably why John's vision still have believers digging shelters in their lawns."

I pussyfooted past the octopus, the bat, and all the other emblems my imagination brought to life at night, until I came to the vending machines. The condom dispenser was tall enough to conceal a door; with legs so low there was no seeing the other side. It had to have housed another product before it was repurposed for the fantasy suites. There are a lot of condoms in the world, with zebra stripes and leopard spots, but not nearly enough variations to fill this thing.

I held my phone to my cheek like I was actually having a conversation. "Rodin's original *Gates of Hell* is on display in Paris. There are seven known duplicates and no known scaled renditions. The odds of one being behind the condom dispenser on the 19th floor of the Oralia are low."

So why was my hand shaking when I peered around the machine?

The dispenser was so close to the wall there wasn't much space to wedge my fingers in. Even then it wouldn't budge. I thought about rocking it back and forth, but I didn't want Stephen finding me in yet another compromising position. So I declared another victory for my rational mind and went back to the room.

THE PROCESS

I PICKED a stack of notecards off the nightstand, charged into the parlor, and started writing:

Card 1: *Break in the routine*

Card 2: *Goal*

Card 3: *Point of no return*

Card 4: *Lowest possible moment*

Card 5: *Climax*

There you have it, every western story every told.

I called Stephen, ordered a cooler full of energy drinks, a roll of tape, and a ball of yarn.

I stuck my notecards on the mural and the strung yarn through them in the shape of an upside-down pentagram, a declaration that I'd concurred Barkley's superstition and I was ready to get shit done.

Cue the writing montage: the fingers blurring over the keyboard, the pocket printer spewing paper, the cumulative stack of pages.

Cut to the pentagram filling with prints: H.R. Giger's portrait of Satan wielding a crucifix like a slingshot, Eliphas Levi's drawing of the goat demon Baphomet, and Rodin's *Gates of Hell.* A series of quick cuts as the strings fill with clips of products Carver insisted upon including.

Cue Stephen bowing in and out, carrying office supplies, steam trays, and toiletries. Cue me waving him in wearing a long Oralia shirt like a nightgown.

Cut to inserts of the counters filling with cans, the table filling with takeout, and ice melting in the bucket.

Cue me pacing the parlor, drink in hand, ranting at the walls like a patient in a padded cell.

Cue me discovering a pair of antlers coming untethered from a piece of furniture. Cue me fastening the antlers to a headband, crouching behind a tree trunk, and jumping out at Stephen.

Barkley Carver enters from the balcony in a saucy stewardess uniform.

Cue the dance number. Barkley and I do the tango. I, of course, take the lead.

Cut to a close up of two crude drawings: one is the shadow demon, with plumes of smoking coming off him, the other is the giant gyroscopic Satan, with eyeballs for skin. Cue my hands smashing them together, making them kiss.

Pan over the pages. Close up on the red lines, the chicken scratch in the margins, and the drawings of cartoon demons.

Cut to Barkley reading pages fresh from the pocket printer on the floor. "Do you think I'll like it?"

Cut to me swinging from the sex swing. "Not at first. You'll think it's too scattered brained, but you'll come around once you see how everything connects in the end."

Cut to a close up of my thousand-yard stare, then a shot over my shoulder of the forest mural. Adjust the focus so the trees appear to be growing while I appear to be shrinking. Cue the night winds, turn them up steady until they're almost deafening. Cut to a breeze wafting over the pentagram. Mute everything.

Cut to me reaching for the wall in a swift jerking movement, as if I'm being yanked forward. Close up on my eyes widening.

At the end of the montage, the question the audience should be left with is: did my fingers touch the wall or go through it?

Fade out.

THE MISSING PAGES

THE TIME HAD COME to treat myself. Draft one was done and I was going to get the most out of Barkley's platinum per diem.

The kitchen's rustic countertops were lined with ice buckets, each filled with a sampling of the finer champagnes the Oralia had in its cellar. Embroidered towels sat beneath them like coasters. The cutting board was brimming with a color swatch of exotic cheeses, and the freezer was dripping with impossible ice cream flavors: wasabi, curry, and avocado.

I picked out a carton of ramen-flavored gelato, twisted the carton, and dug in. The first taste was horrifying. My tongue felt that cool creamy texture and anticipated the fruity tang that usually came with it. What it got was a salty hardy lump of iced chicken broth. My first impulse was to spit it out. My second impulse was to try another bite. My third impulse was to lick the spoon clean.

I held the carton and slid the balcony door open I threw my hands up like a prisoner in a spotlight. I'd pulled an all-nighter, but I hadn't expected Mr. Sun so soon. Los Angeles was at peek brightness. The smog had lifted enough to give the dome of the Griffith Observatory a nice healthy shine.

I gulped another spoonful of gelato down, wondering what I'd think of it had I not warped my taste buds with all the citrus. I licked my fingers, wiped them off, and waved them over my keyboard.

I attached the document to an email to Matilda MacDonald. This manuscript was nothing like the one she'd ordered. I'd taken her notes under consideration, I was still the heroine, but I had given Barkley a Devil worth fearing. I figured if Barkley liked any of the yarns I'd spun around town he was going to love this. But I still couldn't bring myself to hit SEND.

•••

I lingered out on the balcony, soaking up the sun, savoring the last few ramen-flavored scoops from the carton.

I slipped on something on the way back into the room. A newspaper clipping stuck to my foot. It was an advertisement for a widescreen TV, one of the props Matilda insisted I shoehorn into the story. A few more steps and I found an ad for flatbread, then another for hummus dip. I scanned the wall to find the yarn pentagram was gone, as were the notecards, and the satanic prints. All that remained was a pile of advertisements.

"Stephen? You know you have to say 'Housekeeping' before you come in? Right?"

I expected to find him wrapping yarn around his arm, stuffing crumpled wads into his apron, but I was alone.

•••

I checked the wall for impressions of newsprint, red thread, or signs of tape. Whoever had torn the pentagram down did it quick and clean, but still took the time to separate the cryptic clippings from the name brands.

I flipped through the discard pile: fitness fashions, luxury liquors, and gaudy gadgets. Each clipping was punctured in the upper right. The holes were precise, about the size of railroad spikes. They were crumpled in the same way, as if they'd been stuck through and flicked free. I don't remember doing that. Did I do that? I hadn't slept since I finished the first draft. My memory was foggy at best.

Still why the hell would I throw out my own notes?

I tapped my photo app, switched the flashlight on, and went toward the painting looking for signs of tape. I scanned the forest mural, pinched and zoomed, searching for residue.

I waved my phone over the matte painting, marveling over the meticulous design. The trunks were painted in shades of red, ginger, and gold. Enlarged in the viewfinder I saw hints of turquoise, magenta, and cyan mixed into the bark chips. The brushstrokes were so fine that the each leaf was detailed down to the needles. This was clearly a print, but had it been commissioned for this room alone?

I scanned the bottom of the image for the artist's signature. That's where I spotted the yarn. Not a lingering thread clinging to a piece of tape, like I'd expected, but a long red string painted into the scenery itself. There it was trailing off a twig in the foreground. I scanned the cedar chips to find it continued. A tiny little thread no wider than a single bristle ran up into a branch.

I knelt down to search the ground around the thread. I grew up in the desert. I can tell if someone has left impressions in sand, but leaves, especially these strokes were hard to track, but there was something peeking out of the foliage, something that didn't belong. I took a snapshot without thinking and zoomed in.

There it was plain as pixels: the googly-eyed, double

tongued, diaper wearing demon from the pages of the Codex Gigas, complete with the little lines signaling my printer cartridge was almost out of ink.

I'd just had my first experience with sleep paralysis, it was fitting I'd experience sleep deprivation hallucinations soon after.

I tried to slap myself awake, but the horny lizard demon with the raptor talons and lipstick lips was still there in the painting.

I scanned the ground around him and that's where I found the hoof prints, at least four times the size of the page from the Codex Gigas in proportion, tracking one by one, bipedal, like a man. The prints swerved around the trees, over the outlets, and past the vents. I followed them until I came to the balcony, to sunny California and all the shiny happy people holding hands. I threw the sliding doors shut to find the prints continued across their painted surface.

I'd swiped my phone into video mode. The screen panned over the thick primeval roots and the hoof prints that dared to walk beside them. The hooves turned onto a path and trailed off into the distance.

I stepped onto the handcrafted furniture, mulling over the mural, scanning for clues. The end tables moaned as I leapt around, playing a game of hot lava. I lost track of the evidence I'd gathered. Then the phone lost its charge. I backtracked to the sliding doors, but couldn't find a single cloven impression in the dimming light of the room.

I knelt at the outlet, but failed to find my starting point. The printout from the *Codex Gigas* had been painted in the same rusty color tones as the mulch around it, smaller than a thumbnail, sticking partway out. Without magnification, the odds of spotting it again would be like finding a poet in a Cadillac.

•••

I lay beside my phone, waiting for the startup icon. My wall charger was old and off brand. When a current passed through the transistors it made a high-pitched crackling, not unlike leaves rustling. As the LCD screen woke I felt myself starting to drift. The charger buzzed as the battery started sucking juice down. It hummed in and out almost like breathing. A breeze peeled my hair away from my face. I felt something coarse and a wet drag along my cheek.

"I can smell your soul."

Mud, splinters, and eyes like fire. The demon knelt over me, his face as long as my abdomen, his tongue slithering from his mouth. I seized up. My legs sunk into the muck between his hooves.

The demon wrapped his forefinger and his thumb around my neck. His glowing red eyes flared up. They widened in anticipation, only to narrow as the demon's attention was drawn to something else.

"Housekeeping." The door creaked open.

I sat up as Stephen let himself in.

I had to finish that book and get the hell out of that room.

GATHERING INTELLIGENCE

EVERY HAUNTED HOUSE movie has one: the obligatory research scene. A housewife needs to know more about the tragic events that her real-estate agent glossed over. A widow needs to know if the whispers she's hearing are coming from her dead husband. A single mom needs to develop a profile of her son's imaginary friend. Where do they go for this information: the national archives, a grief counselor, or a child psychologist? Nope. These ladies go to the library.

If films have taught me anything it's that when desperate women need information about the supernatural they take a deep dive into the Dewey Decimal system. The Oralia didn't have a library, but they had a gift shop with an extensive newsstand.

I picked up a magazine on the psychological effects of stress, another on dream interpretation, and one on post-modern paganism. The place was a treasure trove. There was even a quarterly whose sole focus was *The History of the Devil.* Of course I could've continued to sift through the Internet, but in my state it was getting harder to tell the signal from the noise.

I hated to admit it, but Matilda was right: seeing something on a shelf made it feel like it belonged there. These periodicals had been curated, edited, and sourced. Any old blogger could have a bad trip and call himself an expert on the occult, but these journalists had to show up to an office, with pants on no less.

In haunted house movies, desperate women set their leather-bound volumes across tables in the darkest corners of the library. They turn the pages, soaking in the etchings until their eyes bug out and their jaws hang open.

I laid my magazines across the bar, ordered a Bloody Mary, and started skimming, running a sharpie under some of the more intriguing passages I found.

I underlined an article titled *Why Most Dreamers are Illiterate*. Turns out, our subconscious minds have trouble holding geometric shapes for any length of time. They can never render text long enough for us to decipher it. Our subconscious minds rarely have the resources to spell things out.

The next passage in the dream interpretation magazine I underlined said *dreams about the Devil are really about temptation*, like the temptation to betray one's morals for short-term monetary gain. Sounded right. I also underlined the phrase *demons can symbolize over-indulgence*, as I poured the last of my drinks down my throat and ordered another.

I tapped the record button on my phone. "If the Devil symbolizes over-indulgence what was Barkley over indulging? Was that the only time Barkley stayed in that room or had he been there with other guests? What was that fight with his wife really about?"

•••

I fished the celery out of my Bloody Mary, nibbled on the

stick, and dug into the periodical about *The History of the Devil.*

There was an article on Anton LaVey; the carnival organist turned satanic priest. LaVey founded the Church of Satan in San Francisco, four miles from Grace Cathedral, where he lived with his wife, children, and a 500-pound lion. The infamous *Black Pope* wore a cloak, horns, and signature pendant: an inverted pentagram with a rendering of the demon Baphomet. LaVey presided over his followers from the bowels of his black house, where he performed baptisms, funerals, and the ultimate affront to goodness — a wedding. Of all these rituals, LaVey never claimed to have raised any Devils. He considered Satanism to be a philosophy, promoting individual freedoms over the church's dated concept of sin. He only invoked the dark lord to troll the opposition. LaVey died in 1997 and his church splintered off into fragments. The black house has been converted into a duplex. It looks quiet charming.

•••

The next article was about a woman named Michelle Smith who was so desperate to ease her depression she tried an experimental treatment called regression hypnotherapy. Michelle's therapist, Lawrence Pazder, suggested putting her in a trance to help recover her traumatic memories. Michelle reverted to her five-year-old self and screamed for 25 minutes straight. Fourteen months and many sessions later Smith knew what had happened to her. She'd been trapped in cage filled with snakes, starved, tortured, and sexually assaulted by her parents. They were members of a cult and they were using their daughter as an offering in a ritual to summon the Devil. Michelle and her doctor chronicled her ordeal and the Satanic Panic of the 1980s began.

People everywhere went into trances and woke up ready to point the finger, and like their counterparts in Salem these people saw witches everywhere. From Miami, Florida to Manhattan Beach, California, the country was awash with accusations of Satanic Ritual Abuse. Victims claimed entire towns were heading into the forest, practicing black masses, forced abortions, and human sacrifices. They alleged that every backcountry road was littered with mass graves. The problem was the victims were claiming more people were sacrificed than had actually gone missing.

Anton LaVey threated to sue Lawrence Pazder for libel for dragging the Church of Satan into Michelle's account. To LaVey's church hadn't been founded at the time Michelle's memories took place. In fact, Michelle claimed her parent's ritual took her out of school for three months, but her elementary school had no record of an absence. Michelle's account continued to fall apart under scrutiny, as did the country's obsession with regression hypnotherapy, which was revealed not to enhance memory but to distort it.

•••

I stretched my arms over my head and let out a long agonizing yawn.

The bartender mirrored my movements. He chuckled. "That's contagious you know."

"Not if you're a psychopath." I fired back.

I rubbed my eyes.

Either an ancient evil had taken up residence in the hotel or I was I having a psychological breakdown. Truth could not find a place to rest between these extremes. It seemed to be leaning toward the theory that everything I'd seen was a dream. This study in demonology taught me more about humanity than the other side. Even the picture from the Gigas Codex, on my phone, started to look like leaves and grass.

I hit the record button in my memo application. "I don't care what Keyser Söze says, the greatest trick the Devil ever pulled was convincing people that an absence of evidence was proof of his existence."

I flipped through the magazine, scanning the depictions of the Devil like a witness searching for a suspect. I found one that almost lined up with the demon in my dreams. It was a broad-shouldered tower of a monster, with horns, hooves, and a beard, but there was something that didn't belong in one of his hands. Pipes, no not pipes, a flute. I thought it odd that the layout editor missed this glaring error before letting it go to print. Unless she thought the Devil and the Greek God Pan were one in the same.

CLEANSING RITUAL

I YAWNED on the way to the elevator. I tasted pickle. I couldn't help but wonder if I drank three Bloody Mary's in here if she'd appear. When I yawned again I lost my balance. When I opened my eyes I found my forehead pressed into the mirror like I'd tried to head butt my reflection.

I called Barkley. I had questions and I needed a distraction from my reflections. My sleep-deprived eyes were creating a funhouse effect. I leaned on my heel and my ass jutted out like a whale. I leaned on my toes and I was skinny as a rail. Self-conscious as I was I about my body I knew I wasn't all that fat or all that skinny. I couldn't see the simple reality that I was drunk.

I spoke into the phone while it was still ringing. "What is it called when it looks like there's only two possibilities, when there's really a third? It's not a false equivalency, but a..."

The logical fallacy was called a false dilemma, when what appears to be a dichotomy is actually a trichotomy or a quadrichotomy or more. It was like saying either aliens have abducted people or they don't exist, and ignoring the possibility that we haven't met them yet. It was like saying I was either an artist or a sellout, and ignoring the possibility that there was an audience that was hungry for what I wanted to make. It was like saying either my room was haunted or my fantasy prone personality was getting the better of me, and ignoring the possibility that...

Barkley picked up on the umpteenth ring. "Noelle. I was just thinking about you."

"You don't say."

"I've been boning up on shadow people all morning."

"You don't say."

"The neurology behind these hallucinations is fascinating. Our amygdalae are programed to perceive any unknown stimuli as a threat. When we're caught between sleep and wakefulness our brains just up and panic. The mind creates theses featureless intruders to justify that sense of terror."

"Interesting."

I knew all this before I checked in, but right now I was wondering what happened to someone who remained between sleep and wakefulness for a week straight. There was a ratcheting sound like Barkley was scrolling through one of those an old-fashioned mouse wheels. "The more I'm reading the more I'm coming around to your theory that the demon was in our minds. I mean I was brought up to believe in angels and exorcisms, but what I saw in the Oralia was probably just a glitch in my sleep cycle. Now that I've gotten that little revelation out of my system, was there something I could help you with?"

I huffed. "Was the fight with your wife over another woman?" There was an artful way to broach the subject, but I was tired, drunk, and my tongue was so loose it was falling out of my mouth.

Barkley's tone shifted. "Why would you ask that?"

I raised an eyebrow at my reflection. "I'm coming around to your theory that it was a demon, but I need to know how he was summoned."

Barkley muttered, "But the neuroscience is so convincing—"

"Oh, it is, but did your wife know you were sleeping with your assistant in that very room?" I squinted at my reflection. I didn't mean to say this hypothesis aloud, but sleep deprivation didn't leave me much in the way of a filter.

The line went dead for half a minute. "If you want to know why I went to bed feeling anxious, yes, my wife had a hunch. Just so you know, all of this information is part of your NDA." All of the good-natured tone had gone out of Barkley's voice. "Is that what you called me to ask?"

I looked to my reflection, feigning worry. "I am so sorry. The nightmares haven't let up since our last conversation. I'm strung out, reading entirely the wrong magazines, convincing myself certain things can summon demons in hotel rooms."

Barkley sighed, muttered something, and snickered. "If demons showed up every time a man slept around they'd have their own tenants' union."

My reflection nodded. "You're right. I know you're right. I just lost my shit wrapping up this manuscript."

Barkley perked up. "Wait, it's finished? Then send it and you won't have to stay there much longer."

"I mean is a story every really finished? I feel like something is still off. I don't know...I'll send it when I get back. See what you think."

"I'll let Matilda know it's coming, and let you know if it is good to go."

I should've been relieved but I wanted to checkout right then. "What time?"

"I don't know. Noon?"

I took out the sharpie I'd been using to mark up the magazines and wrote *12PM* on the web of my hand.

I knew better than to ask if Barkley and his wife had met any of the other conditions needed for a summoning, like the ritual bloodletting...Unless Carver's wife was having her monthly visitor when they reconciled their union. Further prodding would let on how convinced I was the room was haunted, and Barkley would have me relocated to a facility better suited to handle my needs.

Damn it, this book had become more than just a job. It was the type of torment that usually precedes sainthood.

I wanted to ask if I could checkout earlier, but Barkley hung up before I got the chance.

•••

When I returned to the room I tore the sheets off the bed. Sure enough there was a rust-colored stain on the mattress as wide as an inkblot. Barkley Carver had been cheating and it looked like his wife had had her monthly visitor. Two of my hunches were confirmed.

"That would count as a blood sacrifice."

I raised my phone. "How do you remove a bloodstain from a hotel mattress?"

The virtual assistant chimed back. "Hmmm let me think. I found something on the web about 'How to remove a bloodstain from a hotel mattress.'"

"Alright."

I ran an ice bucket under the sink, dumped a box of baking soda in, and mixed it up. Once it was fizzling I poured it on the big brown butterfly Mrs. Carver left on the bed. I waited until it simmered a bit before dabbing it with a cloth. The color tone changed from rust to chestnut brown. I kept scrubbing, but it was no use.

I went out in the hall and found the janitor's closet unlocked and filled an apron with enough cleaning supplies to poison a small village.

I scraped the grains and soaked the remains in hydrogen peroxide. Once the blood stopped bubbling I drenched it in ammonia. Then came the hardcore scrubbing. I scrubbed until my wrists went raw. I scrubbed until my fingers wrinkled and my palms peeled.

There was just no getting rid of the stain. The best I could do was reduce it to a beige butterfly.

I'm not much of an authority on black magic, but I knew that as long as there was a splatter pattern the invocation was still on. So I did what writers do best. I cut the problem out. I found a kitchen knife, drove it into the mattress, and sliced a circle around the stain. I debated shoving the bit of fabric into the garbage disposal or burning it on the stove, but both options ran the risk of blood particles wafting back into the room.

I should have called the front desk and passed Stephen a bag of trash with the fabric, but I just threw it over the balcony. It glided away until an updraft swept it through the neighboring buildings. It rolled end over end until it was gone.

"This room is now cleansed." I proclaimed to the pigeons perched along the building.

I had no idea who my actions were appeasing. Satan, the Greek God Pan, or my own delirium. What mattered was that I'd defused the situation.

I went back to the bedroom to examine the gash I'd made in the memory foam. Odds were someone would feel it through the sheets. I felt around my apron and found the solution. Several strips of duct tape later the evidence was buried beneath the comforter.

It had been an eventful day. I'd accused my benefactor of

cheating, ransacked a janitor's closet, and vandalized a mattress, and it wasn't even afternoon.

Satisfied, I emailed my manuscript and lay on the couch to rest my eyes.

DEVIL-MAY-CARE

WITH MY LUGGAGE packed and ready, I gave Stephen a call. I asked if the kitchen had any of the snack products Barkley had me shoehorn into the manuscript. They did, so I ordered them all. It seemed fitting.

It wasn't long before Stephen wheeled a cart through the door. He couldn't help but notice my luggage in the entryway.

"How is the book coming?"

I nodded. "Done, and if all goes well I'll be out tomorrow morning." I made a show of taking the suite in one last time. The sequoia support beams, the leafy sex swing. I'd been desensitized to the absurdity of it. The room was not without its charm, which had me wondering. "Why hasn't anyone else checked in on this floor since I got here?"

"I didn't tell you?" He pointed to the vines. "All of this is coming out — the murals, the theme rooms, all of it. People just aren't into fantasy like they used to be."

"Oh I'm a writer, you don't have to tell me."

He pointed to the hall. "You got in right before the renovation."

That would explain the project's time restrictions. Barkley

had to sequester a writer up here, because he wouldn't get another opportunity. Matilda had almost convinced me that the man actually liked my work.

My stomach growled. Apart from the Bloody Mary I had for breakfast I hadn't eaten.

Stephen pushed the cart into the kitchen and stacked my order along the counter. My mouth watered at the sight of the containers: a cheese plate, fancy flatbreads, a veggie platter, and several cartons of dip, enough hors d'oeuvres to make for a decent entrée. I was going to miss eating like this when I was slurping down ramen again.

It occurred to me how indebted I was to this man. Stephen had been my personal butler throughout my time here, and whenever he knocked at the door I was too absorbed in my writing to talk about much else. He was always a patient captive audience for whatever scene I was working on. I should've spent some of that time listening to him. Conversations are supposed to be a game of catch. Here I'd been playing dodge ball just hurling my ideas at him.

I shut my eyes tight, wracking my brain for a question worth asking. "What drew you to this line of work?"

Stephen gave that the subtle soundless laugh I'd grown accustomed to. "It's not exactly a calling. It keeps a steady stream of guitar pedals flowing through my apartment, but I don't get much more out of it. Why do you ask?"

"I was curious. Why here? Why the Oralia?"

"There's something dream-like in the air. It's inspiring."

"Do write lyrics here?"

Stephen looked over his shoulder like there was anyone around. He rolled up his sleeve to reveal a tiny memo pad. He held a finger to his lips, "Shhhh."

I smiled like a teenager who just caught her art teacher with a joint. "Read me something."

Stephen chortled. "That's not going to happen."

"Oh but it is."

"They're too personal."

"Then you're definitely reading something."

Stephen scanned his brow trying to follow my logic. He looked back to find me with my arms crossed, tapping my foot, looking to a watch I that wasn't there.

There was a buzzing not too far behind me. I looked over my shoulder to find the sliding door open and my drone friend peeping in. I tripped over my own foot and tugged the door shut. My reflection caught me off guard — eyes all red, lips all white, bedhead all everywhere.

I tugged my hair into a ponytail and tried to tie it into a knot. "You were saying there was something you wanted to read?"

Stephen sighed. "Let's see." He flipped through his memo pad. "This one is short, because it isn't finished—"

"Don't bias my interpretation." I couldn't help but toy with him.

Stephen smirked, scanned his stanza, and recited it without breaking eye contact.

Mirror mirror on the wall
Who is it with all the gal
To glare, gawk, and goggle
With big glowing eyeballs?
Who is it inside the chrome
Who whispers when I'm all alone
Who occupies the oculus
Who's that hiding behind the glass?

Stephen shrugged. "That's all I've got."

I gave that a golf clap. "Did you write that in the elevator?"

Stephen nodded.

I tugged at my collar feeling guilty for planting idea of *The Devil's Toybox* in his head.

"It's cool. I just hope haven't ruined the elevator for you.

We horror writers use mirrors for cheap scares, but they're just surfaces that reflect more light than they absorb. I mean, seriously, if the Devil wanted to come for your soul he'd get you while you were sleeping."

That got Stephen smiling. "That's comforting."

I can't believe I hadn't noticed that he had dimples until right then.

I reached out and took his palm. "Thanks for sharing, thanks for listening to my stories, and thanks being so patient with all my strange requests."

Stephen put a hand to his heart and gave a bow, a gallant gesture if ever there was one. I was starting to get a sense of who he was outside of this. With his hair down, I could see him rocking out on stage, guitar slung over his shoulder, staring out into the audience with those piercing grey eyes.

I tore a page off the hotel stationary, jotted something down, folded it up, and handed it to him. He unfolded it to find my number. That had him blushing more than when I gave him my measurements. I smiled a little too wide and he smiled right back.

I couldn't help but laugh.

I tucked the number into his pocket. "What?"

I sighed. "It's just a shame. Don't you think?"

"What?"

I ran my fingers around my collar. "That this room isn't going to get a proper send off before they tear it apart?"

Stephen gave a quiet contemplative look of slow comprehension.

•••

I fell back on the counter and waved off all of Barkley's product tie-ins to the floor. The wheel of Papka Smoked Gouda rolled across the carpet. The Preston Gourmet Flatbreads spilled out like a deck of cards, and the Natural Meadows Hummus Dip landed with a splat.

I ran the tip of my nose down the length of Stephen's. His lips hovered over mine until I grabbed him by the collar and closed the gap. We kissed. We kissed like lovers returning from war, like teenagers in a closet, like two people who hadn't gotten a piece in entirely too long.

We kissed like we were starving for it.

I ran my fingers down the lengths Stephen's broad shoulders, shamelessly squeezed his biceps, his forearms, and his ass. His lips moved onto my cheek, my chin, and my neck. His breath made my skin feel electric.

I cast my pullover onto floor, revealing one of the bras I'd had him order. I tugged him up onto the redwood counter and unbuttoned his shirt.

I felt for the bulge in his tight uniform pants and knew those had to go. I cast his belt over my shoulder and tugged at his slacks to reveal the thighs of soccer player.

"Damn boy. How often do you take the stares?"

I hooked my fingers through his waistband. Stephen caught them just as I was tugging.

"Do you want to take this someplace a little more hygienic?... Oh fuck..."

Stephen's boxer briefs sagged to his ankles. I'd already gotten my hands on him.

"What did you have in mind?"

"Like the bedroom."

I thought about the mattress with the hole I'd slit in it, the patch made of duct tape. Then I saw something.

"I've got a better idea."

•••

Stephen and I lay naked, in each other's arms, with our

sweat dripping into the carpet. I swatted the sex swing like a lazy cat with a piece of string.

Stephen leaned back and stretched his arms out like he was about to make angels on the carpet. He squinted at the microwave. It blinked 12:00. "Did you turn the clocks off?"

I shrugged. "It's a writer thing."

A phone rang from somewhere deep inside the forest props.

Stephen perked up. "Shit." He raced around the room gathering the pieces of his uniform. With his top half assembled, he spun around trying to find his bottoms.

"A-hem." I cleared my throat.

Stephen turned back wide eyed and spooked.

I pointed upward. His pants were dangling from a rubber vine above him. The phone glowed through the pocket. He had to leap just to catch the bottom hem. I was particularly proud of that throw.

Stephen's phone slid out. He caught it before it hit the floor, shushed me and, tapped the screen. "Yes ma'am... The elevator is doing that thing again, yes... I'll call him when I get back down... I'm on my way down the stairs now." Stephen jerked his pants up. "I'm sorry, you don't know my boss. She thinks I'm a millennial and likes to lecture me about all the problems with my generation."

"Talk about a backhanded compliment." I helped him zip his fly, wrapped my arms around his waist, and kissed him on the lips. "Call me?"

Stephen gave that single confident nod. "Like *call* call? Not text?"

I nodded.

He flashed that big perfect smile. "We could go on a date."

"Play your cards right and I might let you get to second base."

We kissed goodbye, a pair of strangers, who actually kind of knew each other.

Once Stephen was gone I realized there was one last souvenir I had to have, especially now that the Oralia had no further use for it.

The sex swing was linked to the ceiling with a pair of snap hooks, the kind that open if you apply a little bit of pressure to the hinge. I stood on the coffee table, used a mop and a broom handle like tongs, and unlatched the hooks one at a time. I had no clue how I'd mount the swing in my apartment, but it felt like such a shame to let it go to waste, especially now.

As I coiled the vine around my arm I realized there was no space left in my luggage. That's when I remembered the pocket in my trench coat. At least I could take a little piece of the Oralia home with me.

•••

Back in my bedroom I picked up the remote, tapped the CH + button through a series of NOT IN SERVICE stations until I found the screen filled with giant redwoods. The speakers crackled with those not so relaxing forest sounds.

I tapped my phone. "What is it about the woods that people find so frightening. Not the animals. Not the lack of modern conveniences. It's something else. Something primal."

My phone vibrated. I was so startled I lost my grip. Matilda's name showed up on the caller ID. I took a moment to catch my breath before hitting *TALK*.

Matilda was well into the conversation before I could say anything.

"You were supposed to give us a peek into the abyss, not chronicle your own existential crisis. We wanted Stephen King not Charlie Kaufman."

"Slow down. What are you talking about?"

"I'm talking about this mind fuck memoir we didn't order."

This was not how I imagined this conversation going. I backed into the headboard, scattered veggies everywhere, and smeared the last of the hummus on the covers.

I rubbed my forehead. "Okay, I know there was a difference of opinion on the direction, but this is psychological horror. It's supposed to get intimate and weird."

Matilda had an answer primed for that. "That's your excuse for all your loose ends, it's psychological horror so it doesn't have to make sense?"

Writing a psychological thriller is a lot like an algebra equation:

Setup + Misdirection × Twist/Climax = Satisfy Conclusion.

I'd thought my math was correct, but Matilda had me wondering if all my self-talking and forth wall breaking had unbalanced the equation. Psychological thrillers are supposed to pose the question: *Is something supernatural happening or is it entirely in the hero's mind?* By winking at the audience I skewed that balance so far toward the psychological I couldn't make the demon convincing for a moment.

Matilda rustled through her notes. "Readers are supposed to wonder if the hero is losing her mind, but she's talking to herself long before shit goes down. You spoil the setting by giving her an imaginary friend. When the demon does show up there's no body count, no stakes, and no doubt it's all in her head."

There was a crinkling on the other end. Matilda had notes to cover her criticisms.

"You reveal something supernatural is happening when your hero finds the remains of the other ghostwriters Barkley has lured to the floor, but you double back and say it was all in her head. If it's all in her head, why do the stairs loop back to the 19th? Is she just running in place? You make no effort to answer that before hurling her into a big gapping plot hole.

And what's the moral supposed to be? Selling out always ends in ruin? Trust me kiddo, it doesn't."

I dumped the last of veggies in the dip container and covered it. "What does Barkley think?"

"What I tell him to." Matilda scoffed.

"What did you tell him to think?"

"That someone who spends her time in his employ digging up blackmail material isn't someone he should be in business with."

"Blackmail material?" I hadn't seen this twist coming.

"Someone on staff must've told you they saw Barkley and I getting cozy. You did the math, and accused him of having an affair, hoping to double your advance. The only problem with your plan was you didn't reckon Barkley and his wife might have an arrangement."

"If Barkley has an open relationship, why didn't he mention it?"

Matilda tore something on her end. "Maybe it's the stigma people like you keep perpetuating. You shouldn't be so closed-minded. LA is the Polyamory capitol of the world. You'd know that if you went outside once in a while."

"You paid me not to." My shoulders straightened, my fists curled, and my nails dug into my palms. "You're just trying to back out of our agreement."

Matilda scoffed. "You signed a non-disclosure agreement. I didn't sign a thing."

"We had a verbal contract."

"One you broke when you threw out the outline. Goddamn it Noelle. I've worked with a lot of primadonnas. Most of them think they're going to be the next J.K. Rowling, but you don't have any of those delusions. Do you? That's why you tried to blackmail Barkley. You already knew you were a fraud."

My nails cut into my lifeline. "You can try to weasel out of our agreement, accuse me of extortion, but attacking my integrity as an artist, that's some bullshit."

Matilda cackled. "If you had one iota of artistic integrity then what the hell are you doing up there?"

I didn't have a comeback for that. I was too busy thinking about the producer who thought the worst tragedy he could imagine was a studio turning my script into a film, about my coworkers turning to their phones when I pitched stories in the break room, about the boyfriend who pretended to listen to my story only to forget every detail when it came up again.

"That's what I thought." Matilda mused. "We owned you the moment you checked into that room."

I wanted the money, sure, but what I needed was the validation the money represented; the validation that meant a lifetime of artistic pursuits had not been in vain. For that I was willing to name drop products. For that I was willing to put Barkley Carver's name on the cover. For that I was willing to sell my soul.

THE ONLY WAY OUT IS THROUGH

MATILDA SAID some things about blacklisting the name Noelle Blackwood in her circles, making it impossible for me to find work in a town it was already impossible to find work in, but I couldn't hear her over the crickets chirping. The TV had turned up to maximum volume like it was competing, like Matilda was making the forest angry until its sounds drowned out the speakerphone.

I hit the CH + on the remote, but nothing happened. I hit CH -, still nothing. I hit the power button.

Matilda shouted. "Where the hell are you? Are you even in the Oralia?"

I crawled over the hummus plate, leapt at the TV set, and hit the power button. Nothing happened. I ripped the plug from the outlet and the lights went dark. The chirping remained, but Matilda's voice, the TV, and the AC all went.

•••

My feet sunk into a mulch of pinecones, cedar, and soil. Ancient redwoods, as wide as houses and as tall as skyscrapers towered over me. Moisture licked my skin as a musty odor filled the air.

I craned my neck. The canopy was glowing with fireflies. They weaved in and out of the trees in a helix formation. The branches flashed with their little red bomb blasts.

I shook my head, hoping to feel a pillow beneath it. I stretched my arms, hoping to feel a headboard above me. I rubbed my eyes, hoping to awaken in the room with the moon shaped lantern, but the forest remained.

I was about to pinch myself when I noticed something.

The article I'd read on dreams said the brain has trouble maintaining geometric shapes when it's unconscious. That's why locations change whenever you turn around. That's why faces swap mid conversation. That's why you can't check your watch or read a street signs. Letters and numbers are illegible.

I wanted to believe this was a dream, but when I looked at my hand it still read *12PM*. The text never wiggled, never bled, or turned to hieroglyphs. It remained solid. This was my real hand. This was really happening. The fireflies. The trees. All of it was real.

A blanket of fog spread across the forest floor. It swerved through the trees and converged on me, blotted out my vision, and clogged my sinuses. It stunk like rotten eggs.

My natural instinct was to run and find cover. I tried to crawl out of the mulch, but my limbs spurned my commands. My knees locked up, my hips failed to swivel, my arms refused to swing.

There was something in the fog. The tingling sensation I felt the first time I was here surged through my limbs. My circulation weakened. My lungs struggled to draw breath. Soon I'd be as stiff as a department store mannequin. The writing on my hand told me I was awake, but the effects of sleep paralysis were setting in. The fog acted as a magical neural toxin, wrapping me up in a psychic spider web.

I writhed in the muck like a hog trying to flip itself over. I shook my head, opened my fingers, and wiggled my toes. Circulation again. I nodded until I could bang my head, flicked my wrist until I could punch, and curled my toes until I could kick. I coughed the toxins out of my system. When the tingling sensation passed, I wrenched myself off the ground and fled the fog.

My pajama bottoms sagged as I went. They were covered in hummus, leaves, and woodchips. The fog looped back around. The path filled with smoke. I cupped my mouth.

The branches blurred in and out of focus. There was something red entangled in the needles. I reached out and felt a familiar texture. Holding it close I saw a long piece of yarn, like the one I'd used to make my notecard pentagram. It fluttered off into the distance.

There was a whistling behind me, like something out of an old western, like when gunslingers' hands danced over their holsters. The fog was too thick to see where it was coming from. All I knew was that it was getting closer.

The yarn was flowing in the opposite direction. So I followed it. The string ran through the branches like power lines and all my little notecards stuck out of the mulch beneath it.

I pressed on, but the whistling behind me grew stronger. Each note wandered the scale searching for a tune. The tone reminded me of the Peruvian flutists selling cassettes on my old college campus. I staggered in the opposite direction, grabbing fistfuls of yarn, and wrapping it around my wrist to cover my tracks. It wasn't long before I found my way out of the fog.

The yarn weaved around saplings and shrubs toward the base of a bluff where it led straight into a cave. The bluff was too steep to mount, the path too foggy to chance, and the cave too dark to trust. It didn't matter which direction I chose. I was about to make a bad decision.

The whistling decided for me. The tempo hastened as the flutist drew closer.

I ran.

•••

The mouth of the cave grew wider. Its archway was lined with stalactites that hung like teeth. Its floor was slick with clay as pink as a tongue. The moonlight shined down its throat giving the impression of a vast tunnel system, but it faded the deeper I went in. I came to the end of the yarn, which had been strung through a rock. I discarded the buildup from my forearm and pressed on blind.

The whistling echoed off the walls, but I'd put a fair amount of distance between the flutist and myself.

I felt around the dark inching toward the source of the splashing. The muck squishing between my toes told me I was getting closer and something in the air was telling me I was getting warmer, literally warmer. Beads of sweat ran down my forehead, streaked down my cheeks, and dripped off my chin.

When I came around a corner my vision returned. At first there was just a dull white blur. Then came the cool blue surfaces, and the hints of red. Skylights shined beams across the cavern, revealing an area the size of a gymnasium. A stream swerved through the bright spots. Bubbles pooled in the craters beside it, boiling in the moonlight. These hot springs weren't fit to be waded in.

Tall stalks of grass stretched for a surface they would never reach. Lights blinked between their blades like cinders rolling off a bonfire. This was where the fireflies had gone off to.

The whistling returned, amplified by the cavern, there was no knowing what direction it was coming from.

The flutist was no longer blowing at random. They'd found a melody, an eerie funeral waltz they played with a virtuoso's proficiency. Still the meter was odd and the song had no clear key. The flutist was bending notes all over the place, punctuating every measure with long vibratos. This was the melody of madness, a soundtrack for things that happened in the cellars of old black houses.

I had no intention of facing the music so I edged along the wall. I hugged the stones, feeling for handholds as I went. Each step was a walk on a tight rope. One foot inched forward while the other tapped it on the heel. One slip and I'd find myself broiling in the hot spring.

The flutist shifted his instrument from its lowest notes to the ear splitting end of the audible spectrum. The song was reaching the crescendo, heralding the coming of a dark cosmic entity.

Steam spurt out in time with the music. I hugged the rock face as droplets sizzled my skin. Blisters erupted across the knuckles of my toes, like hotdogs bursting on a grill. I fought off a scream for fear of revealing my location and pressed on. I did not want to find out where that music was coming from.

It wasn't until I neared the edge of the stream when I saw something that made me question the path I was on. It was a page I'd printed from the *Codex Gigas*. Beside it was a statue, a recreation of the demon with the twin tongues, scale bathing cap, and horn skinned diaper. Someone had chiseled it from the cavern walls and set a pan flute in the demon's hand.

I passed another page I'd printed to inspire my writing: occultist Eliphas Levi's drawing of Baphomet, the Sabbatic Goat.

Beside it was another statue. This Baphomet sat with a crown of fire between his horns, a long beard between his breasts, large black wings, Latin tattoos on his forearms, and a pair of snakes wrapped around the rod that stood in for his erection. He pointed to a moon just over his shoulder. At least that's what he was supposed to be pointing to. Someone had set a pan flute in his hand instead.

A few steps further I found statue of H.R. Giger's Satan. This depiction hid behind a cloak of shadows. Its only features were horns, pointed ears, and a lone eyeball.

In the printout Satan held a crucifix out to the viewer. He tugged on a slingshot he'd threaded through Christ's wounds. In the sculpture the crucifix had been replaced with yet another pan flute.

The whistling swelled followed by the rhythmic clip clop of hooves on stone. The flutist had entered the cavern.

I came close enough stream to see where it was flowing. It ran down a tunnel that led straight out to the woods. I hugged the corner, tiptoed onto dry rock, and entered the tunnel.

The wall across the stream was covered in cave paintings. These were not primitive hieroglyphs. They were fan art, reproductions of Satan and his minions, some I'd printed others I hadn't. There was Henry Fuseli's *Nightmare*, William Blake's *Satan Exulting Over Eve*, and even that horny little Devil from the condom packaging. Each one featured the same artistic addition: the flute in the subject's hand.

And I got it, starring at each flute, Christians had coopted Pan, corrupted his image, and demonized him for generations. When Pan saw what they'd done he didn't take offense. He liked it. To a God starving in obscurity any attention was good attention.

And the demon in the hotel, it was Pan all along.

The clip clopping in the cavern sped to a gallop. Something splashed through the stream behind me. Fireflies swarmed through the tunnel in a flickering blur. I followed them outside into the cool open air and ran for the trees. I had no clue if I was anywhere near civilization. All I knew was I had to put more distance between the whistling and myself.

When I reached the grove I realized it was not as thick as it had appeared. The trees in this gully were so tall they created the illusion that the terrain ahead was even, but in reality there was a bluff running all the way around the tunnel. There were three rows of giant sequoias hiding a wall of moss. The rest of the orchard continued up on the cliff.

I was trapped. Pan had played the piper and herded me into a dead end.

I scanned my surroundings. The branches were too high to reach. There was a redwood, thick as a rocket, leaning against the cliff. I thought to scurry up it, like a desperate cat, but there was no way I was getting any traction at the angle it was resting.

The whistling swirled out from the tunnel. The flutist blew a measure of fast arpeggiated notes, in total command of his instrument.

That's when I saw a dugout beneath the uprooted tree, almost as wide as the cave itself.

The echo of hooves on stone got shorter and shorter. He was almost here.

I slid into the dugout and crawled into the dirt with the spiders and the worms.

I watched the tunnel, waiting to see the flutist in action.

A pair of fireflies hovered in front of me. I tried to shoo them off for fear they'd reveal my location, but they were stubborn. They only came closer.

The fireflies flared up as bright as embers. It took my focus a second to adjust. I saw not insects but a pair of blood red irises— this was Pan staring back.

He'd lured me into his home, through the bathroom, past the art gallery, and into his kitchen. Stupid me had crawled right into the oven.

Even with Pan's natural camouflage I had no idea how I missed him coming. He stood so tall his horns grazed the branches. His vein-riddled biceps shined in the moonlight. Droplets dripped off his wooly legs and sizzled on the grass.

Pan raised the flute, blew the last measure of his funeral song, and shook his pipes, dragging the final note out as long as his lungs could manage. Then he put the flute in his satchel, grabbed me by my sleep shirt, and hoisted me out of the foxhole. My collar dug into my armpits as he lifted me to eyelevel.

Pan's ruby red eyes set his face aglow, revealing its twisted dimensions. His nose was as sharp as a toucan's beak, his beard as untamed as a lion's mane, and his horns curled around his skull and jut out in front like tusks.

He smiled with a mouth full of shark teeth. "I can smell your soul." He licked his lips. "Now I will taste it."

I wiggled to no avail and screamed.

Pan's tongue uncoiled down the length of his beard, slithered toward my face, and drew a ring around my muzzle. It felt like sandpaper as it breached my lips. I gritted my teeth to keep it from burrowing all the way inside my mouth. I could feel it digging beneath my incisors, trying to pry my jaw open, but I jerked away before it could get in.

I grabbed Pan by the horns, dug my heels into his chest, and pushed. He held firm so I cocked my leg back, roared as loud as I could, and kicked him in his big hairy balls.

Pan doubled over.

I scrambled to my feet and darted into the trees, the twigs tearing into my feet, with nowhere to go but back the way I came.

Pan rammed his knuckles into the forest floor, sprang back up onto his hooves, and ran. The ground quaked as he came. When I saw his claws reach over my head I zigzagged to avoid them. He had the leg span, but I had four years of soccer camp on him.

I tried to lose Pan in the trees and run to the gully, where I saw light on its far side. The light took shape the closer I came, like a window in a tree. I ran for it without thinking what was on the other side. All I knew was I'd fit and he would not.

Pan abandoned the tunnel to close the gap between us. I ducked just in time to avoid taking a branch to the abdomen.

I spun around, and tugged the branch as far back as I could. Pan was sprinting before he realized my intentions. The branch swept his hooves out from under him. He took the fall on the chin. He screamed and my ears rung.

The forest spun, but I pressed on toward the light. I ran harder when I saw the mattress on the other side. I leapt headlong at the trunk, dove through the TV, and belly-flopped back into the hotel room.

I scurried around to find Pan was back up on his hooves. He leered at my escape route, sizing it up. When he howled the speakers crackled and stomped the screen flickered. When he blew smoke the image swirled in digital artifacts. Smeared redwoods and Technicolor pixels.

Even when the screen was awash with glitches Pan's glowing red eyes remained at the center.

I groped around the TV set to find the buttons still had no effect. I felt along the carpet to find the cord was still unplugged.

I reached for the remote and pushed every last button. The lights flashed, but nothing happened. "It's useless."

The screen began tracking on its own. Random pixels realigned.

I shook the remote. "What the hell are you doing?"

Remember that movie The Ring? Fear whispered in my ear.

The digital soup churned back into the shape of a faun. Pan knelt into a starting position, tilted his horns, and charged at the screen.

I flipped the remote around and stabbed the glass. A web

of cracks shot out from the point of impact. The image fractured into a row of vertical lines. When I pried the remote out I noticed something had breached the screen from the other side. It was as jagged as a stalactite and as black as night. It was the tip of one of Pan's horns. I chiseled at the glass until the horn broke off.

Sparks shot from the screen, the casing shook, and the speakers rumbled. The vertical lines flickered, changed color, and reformed back into Pan.

Barkley appeared in the room, slid over the mattress, and knocked the TV off the stand. He kicked it in until there was nothing but shards. Then he poured the ice bucket on the remains.

CRYSTALLOMANCY

I SAT THERE FROZEN, contemplating the broken TV, trying to figure out what just happened.

"It's a form of Crystallomancy."

I turned to find Barkley clutching his chest. He wore a flight suit with aviator shades and a popped collar, like a bad Halloween costume of Tom Cruise in *Top Gun*. He was winded. "You know, mirror magic."

I gave that the slow nod of skepticism and mustered a, "And I know that how?"

I was done writing. Why was I seeing him?

Barkley shrugged. "You read it in one of those magazines at the bar. Don't you remember?" He raised a finger as he recited from memory. "The witches of Thessaly used mirrors to invoke the horned god of the forest. Once summoned, any reflective surface near the invocation became an entrance to his realm."

I cast off my soiled sweatpants and swapped them for a pair of jeans. "I've never heard of the witches of wherever, but I'm not sticking around to admire their handy work."

I laced my shoes, more concerned with self-preservation

than I was getting to the bottom of Barkley's summoning. All I knew was that the forest realm was real, the writing on my hand had told me so, and I was not about to get sucked back into it ever again.

Barkley pried the lamp from the nightstand, took it into the bathroom, and broke all the mirrors.

I couldn't help but wonder why the sound of the glass shattering was so piercing. If Barkley was just a projection of my imagination then shouldn't I have felt those impacts on my palms? If I was the one swinging the lamp then shouldn't I have felt a strain on my shoulders? Shouldn't I have seen cuts on my forearms?

All I felt was the hemp lines of my shoelaces. I checked the soles of my sneakers. There was no glass dust to be found. How could I be in the bathroom and the bedroom at once?

I reached across the mattress, shook out my sweatpants and watched the woodchips scatter across the carpet. "How are you doing that?"

"You're doing it." Barkley called back.

"And the TV?"

"All you baby, you and the remote."

I felt the tension in my chest seize up. "Barkley, why are you gaslighting me?"

Barkley came back with a sleeve full of silver dust and set the lamp sideways on the nightstand. He wiped the sweat from his forehead. His smile accented his anger more than it concealed it. "What do you mean *gaslighting*?"

"Seriously Barkley. Just tell her. You don't have much time." Matilda spoke up. She was still on speakerphone. She hadn't hung up yet. For all I knew I was in Pan's realm for but a moment, and Matilda had been listening the entire time.

"What...the...actual...fuck?"

Barkley giggled. "Uh-oh. Here comes that third act twist."

I scooped the phone off the bed. "You can hear him?"

Matilda sighed. “Of course I can, I’m the one who sent him.”

“In a flight suit?” I scoffed.

Matilda snickered to herself. “We figured the wackier he appeared the more likely you’d think he was an agent of your neurosis.”

“You posed as my imaginary friend?” I shook my head. “The logistics of that are insane.”

Barkley shrugged with his palms, an unrepentant child who’d been caught in a lie. Whoever this man was, he was there and he was real. He’d been coming and going into the room the entire time.

I was still shaking my head. “You hired me to write a novel just to tear it apart?”

Barkley nodded. “The horned god is an emotional being. He only responds to strong ones.”

Matilda added, “We had to keep triggering you to lure him out. Nothing personal, but we would’ve been hard on whatever you sent us.”

“Who are you people?”

Barkley cut me off. “It doesn’t matter. What matters is that we get to the last mirror in time.”

“Then what are you talking for? Go.” Matilda hung up.

Barkley grabbed me by the wrist to check the time on my phone.

I shook my head, still dumbfounded, still in denial. “This is all a dream. I need to wake up.”

Barkley nodded as he led me out of the room.

I kept shaking my head. “I was asleep when Pan came to me.”

Barkley tilted his head back and forth. “Or you were and he woke you.”

“But I remember waking up.”

“Or Pan lost his grip on this reality and you mistook

returning for waking up." Barkley spun his hands. "Pan is still finding his bearings. You see trans dimensional travel is a lot like sex. The more you do it the longer you can last."

I wasn't nuts. It was the situation that was bat-shit crazy.

Barkley walked backward with no fear of tripping. He had an eerie familiarity with the suite. "The horned God is allusive. He observes no festivals, has no shrines, and doesn't come when summoned, not unless you offer him something he really really wants."

I was puzzled. Were we actually talking about Greek mythology?

"But Pan is the God of shepherds and flocks. How the hell did he turn so feral?"

Barkley smirked. "It's been a while since he's been with someone. He's pent up. I figured you'd be perfect. He likes creative types, both men and women (hence the term Pansexual). Matilda and I tried to lure him out by channeling the raw hedonism of this room, but he just wasn't that into us."

Barkley honed in on the balcony doors.

I scanned the parlor like a cop checking corners. "If you knew he was so pent up, then why summon him?"

Barkley threw his arms up, turned back, and sneered. "To end two-thousand years of unlawful impersonation."

I opened the closet and threw my coat over my shoulders. It took me a moment to recall why it felt so lopsided. Barkley seized on the distraction. He blocked my exit and herded me back into the room.

"Pan's been sustaining himself on unearned attention. It's high time for that gravy train to end."

"What are you talking about?"

Barkley pushed me closer to the sliding doors. "The same thing I've been talking about all along: brand misappropriation. Why do you think I kept challenging you to come up with a better Devil than the one I'd written?"

I shook my head. "You wanted me to find the one with all the eyeballs."

Barkley tapped his nose. "That's what you should've seen on that expired condom."

"That's Lucifer, Beelzebub, Satan, the King of Babylon, the great deceiver?"

Barkley rolled his eyes. "He has many names. It's part of his branding problem."

Barkley backed me into the glass doors, the last reflective surfaces left in the suite. This was where Pan had crept into the room to tear the yarn off the wall.

Barkley slid one door open. "What's going on between Satan and Pan is much like our arrangement. You write the story, I print my face on the back, hardly seems fair. Now imagine centuries of that. My master does the dirty work only to get depicted in Pan's likeness. Pan owes us worship royalties."

Barkley was physically imposing, but I wondered how light on his feet he'd be if I just made a run for it. I charted a path to the exit.

Barkley positioned himself to grab me if I tried to flee.

"You're not real. None of this is happening."

"Keep telling yourself that."

Barkley slid the glass door shut, knelt down, and examined the mural on its surface. "You'll find out what's real soon enough."

I buckled my coat. "No, I'm getting the fuck out of here."

Barkley grabbed my shoulders. His grip was stronger than I'd anticipated. "You might have trouble getting out the way you came."

I had flashes of my manuscript. My ending featured a bottomless elevator shaft and the fire stairs that looped around forever. It turns out my subconscious had been trying to tell me something, not with an imaginary version of Barkley, or even my dreams, but through my writing.

I looked to the door then back the balcony. “How are you planning on escaping?”

Barkley pointed a finger toward the ceiling to signal he needed a moment to think. “Wait, where’s the sex swing?”

“Are you serious?” I popped my collar and buttoned the top few buttons.

Barkley waved at the glass. “I was going to use it slow him down.” He pushed the coffee table against the balcony doors and checked the mural again.

The fog was so thick there was no telling where the tree line ended and the sky began.

Barkley sidestepped the glass and pushed me forward, presenting me to the forest I’d just escaped.

A dark splotch cut through the fog, and grew into the all too familiar shape of Pan. He ran with perfect form, an Olympian in every sense of the word.

I struggled in Barkley’s clutches, writhing and kicking to no avail, and then he just lost his grip. I fell flat on the floor.

Pan dove through the doors like they were made of air. He vaulted over the coffee table, skewered Barkley and pinned him to the wall. One of Barkley’s lungs popped like a tire, his eyes rolled back, and his mouth hung open in a twisted smile.

Pan punched through the wall, gripped the hole, and lifted his legs. With his hooves pressed to the bricks he sprung off and kicked. He broke through like a wrecking ball, flattening the wall between the parlor and the bedchamber.

THE RED CAULDRON

I RAN like hell down the hall. I didn't bother calling the elevator because somehow I knew it had been transformed into a bottomless pit.

The floor rumbled. I lost my footing, and slammed my shoulder into an octopus knocker. I didn't have time to examine the impression it left in my arm. Something had already chimed behind me.

I looked back to find Pan had skewered the knocker for my room. His one remaining horn stuck through the door. He took great care to wiggle this horn free without snapping it off.

That was the only head start I was ever going to get. I veered toward the stairwell, but somehow I knew it would only loop onto itself.

I had one option.

I went for the condom dispenser. I tried rocking it back and forth. It budged, but refused to tip. I wedged myself into the gap, kicked off the wall, and threw my back into it. The machine crashed.

And there it was: the big black door from my dream, the ninth cast of Rodin's *Gates of Hell.*

The door opened on its own.

There was movement in the darkness: flashes of firelight, wooden cranks, and chains.

I knew this path led straight to a slip and slide, a cauldron, and certain incineration, but staying in the hall meant incurring the wrath of Pan.

The ground shook again. Fixtures shattered on the floor, lose bulbs swung from the ceiling. Dust and debris rained down.

Pan howled.

I glanced back as the door to my room embedded itself in the opposite wall. Pan was too big to fit through the frame. He tried ducking, but his shoulders were too broad. He threw an arm at the archway until it burst.

Pan shuffled into the hall hoof over hoof like a hockey player skating sideways. He crashed into the door and it burst into a pile of kindling. Cracks shot out across the wall, breaking the housing for the fire extinguisher, which wobbled to the floor.

In one angry gesture Pan shook the sawdust from his mane, the paint chips from his hair, and the splinters from his hand. His eyes honed in on me.

I ran into the dark, zigzagging through the torture devices that lined the entryway: the iron maiden, the Judas Cradle, the Catherine Wheel. All the spikes, hooks, and blades, came just shy of piercing my flesh. To make matters worse ropes rose from the cobblestones like trip wire. Had it not been for the firelight I'd have gone down a few steps in.

A line of torches whizzed by through a mechanism in the ceiling. I followed them out of the entryway, through the archway, and into the great cosmic cathedral. I walked out onto the landing. Not a place I wanted to be when Pan came in.

Banners of flesh unfurled from the walls. Blood spewed through the brickwork of skulls in violent torrents.

A web of ropes led from the archway to the dome ceiling. The cathedral echoed with the screeching of a thousand pulleys all winding at once. The way I'd come from erupted with the screams of the damned. I rolled out of the way. A hanging cage slid past me dragging sparks along the cobblestones. It rose up to the ceiling like a chandelier. The poor soul inside shook the bars. His suffering was reduced to a prop for my benefit. Another cage followed then another, each one rising to a perch somewhere above the landing.

Satan's cathedral was still assembling itself.

Pan's hooves echoed across the stones. He was trapped in the entryway, swatting at cages as they passed. He roared so loud my ears rang again. He might have made me lose my balance if I wasn't already air born.

I had tackled a cage and threaded my arms through the bars before it lifted from the ground. It yanked me hard. I yelped, much to the surprise of the poor soul inside, a toothless, tongue less, mummy of man with wild milky eyes. The rope jerked and the cage took flight. I was throttled. My grip shifted from the top rung to the second.

Firelight passed like stars. The force of the pull shifted. The cage veered from a horizontal to a vertical motion and we swung like a pendulum.

The soul inside the cage recoiled at the sight of me. He turned away, shrieking until a long string of drool trickled down his chin. He tried to shake me but his wiry legs couldn't muster the strength.

When the cage came to a complete stop my palms were blistered, my arms were strained, and my coat was ripped through the armpits. The sex swing hadn't felt so heavy when I wound it up, but now it felt like it was made of lead tubing.

A Judas cradle flew across the landing, followed by an iron maiden, and a Catherine wheel, which rolled down several steps before ultimately shattering.

Pan was slow to enter the cathedral. He crawled through the archway with his tail on high alert. Still on all fours, he scanned the platform, and sniffed the air. The cathedral was rife with the smell of charred cinder, sulfur, and burnt flesh. I prayed that the interference made it harder for him to isolate my scent.

With Pan in the room, the floor felt closer. The fall seemed safer. He skewed my perspective. Next to him the mastodonic support beams looked like elephant bones, the skulls looked like doll heads, and the torches looked like matchsticks.

Pan scanned his surroundings. He was oblivious of the coliseum steps, the cathedral, and pit of fire at the center. He was on the hunt. Nothing else mattered.

Pan shifted his gaze to the ceiling. The prisoners shuffled in their cages, hissed and spat as he passed beneath them. The horned god roared right back. He didn't care whose court he was on. He wasn't leaving until the trophy was in his hands.

I climbed around the cage to avoid detection. The soul inside shifted to avoid my touch.

I heard mocking laughter over my shoulder. "She got you too, huh?"

A man in the nearest cage smirked at me. He seemed healthier than the others, like he'd just gotten there. I knew his sharp Nordic features. His combed grey beard and slicked back hair were all familiar. This was the Hollywood producer who'd shamed me out of the industry; the one who said the real tragedy was that someone might actually make my movie.

This couldn't have been a coincidence.

He leered through his bars. "I take it Matilda offered you a three picture deal?" The producer twirled his zippo between his fingers like a gambler with a poker chip. This was the same lighter with the Sigil of Baphomet. He held it out so I could examine the inscription on the bottom.

With Love my pet,

Matilda

The producer almost dropped it when a brick hit him in the shoulder.

Pan was lobbing cobblestones at random, rattling cages, and trying to knock them down.

When the producer glanced back he found me prying the zippo from his hand.

"Got a light?"

I snatched the lighter, climbed the top of my cage, and leaned back over.

Pan leapt up and down crushing more cobblestones, making more ammunition. He was pent up. He was taking his frustrations out on his audience. He wasn't going anywhere near that cauldron without a reason.

I had to give him one.

I grabbed the rope suspending the producer's cage, flicked Matilda's gift open, and set his rope aflame.

Pan marched to the wall, pried a torch out, and lit the nearest banner. It went up fast. By the time he ignited the next one the first had burned down to the mast. Then he went down the line burning everything on the platform until every banner was engulfed.

The souls whose cages were in the line of fire cried out in agony and ecstasy.

The producer climbed his cage, stretched through the bars, and reached for the suspension cable. He tried to smother the flame with his bare hands, but it had grown too high and now it was licking the ceiling.

Desperate, the producer swung his cage back and forth. He leaned in my direction attempting to clutch the bars I was standing on, but it was too late. His rope had gone black and dissolved to ash.

"You lousy bitch."

I nodded. “I may not be likeable, but I’m resourceful.”

The producer plummeted and his cage shattered on impact. The base cracked, the rings shot up, and the bars scattered everywhere.

The producer’s feet exploded and his calves crinkled up like cans of red spray paint. There was so much blood amidst all the rust, it was hard to tell where his injuries ended and the wreckage began. Still, the producer found the strength to crawl toward the coliseum steps and hurled himself over the edge.

Pan turned toward the commotion and followed the blood trail down. His tongue slithered out of his beard, arched up, and tasted the fear on the air. It didn’t take long before he found its source.

Pan’s glowing red eyes locked onto his target. The producer let out a cowardly scream. He rolled down the steps and Pan followed, stepping hoof over hoof, never noticing the bubbling cauldron in the center of the room.

The producer landed on his back just as Pan stomped his groin flat. The poor bastard burst like a ripe tomato. He didn’t scream so much as he let the last gasp of air from his lungs.

Pan gripped the producer by the throat, held him high, and drove the torch into his torso, all the way up into his guts. The producer’s head glowed until his eyes popped and smoke billowed from the sockets.

When Pan discarded the producer’s body it kept right on burning. He had cooked it from the inside out. Satisfied, Pan danced around the flames, a tribesman in a brand new ritual. Not only had Pan liked seeing himself as the Devil, he liked casting judgment on sinners as well.

The cathedral rumbled as the architecture transformed. The top row of the coliseum steps tilted downward, then the next, and the next. Pan discarded his torch only to find it slide back a newly formed ramp. The domino effect knocked Pan off his hooves, sending him hurtling toward the cauldron. He'd fallen into Satan's trap.

The pit erupted as a mushroom cloud shot straight up. The cages inside the blast radius were burnt to a crisp. The lava painted the dome a shade of blood orange. I felt the heat on my skin.

A thunderous whooshing echoed throughout the dome. Then came the familiar metallic clinking of a great chain raising a platform.

The cauldron spilled over with a great lake of lava. Four wheels emerged from the center, each as long and wide as off-ramps. They swirled in a gyroscopic motion, churning through the lava like an eggbeater. The cages creaked with each rotation.

Each of Satan's faces rose from the whirlpool. The eagle, the lion, the bull, and the man. Their features blurred like monuments in the distance, revealing the grandeur of the cathedral and the staggering titan who called it home.

A pair of batwings splashed through the magma. In a few swift movements, the whole of Satan was hovering over the flames. Lava dripped from the eyeballs that coated his muscles. Each pupil honed in on the dot sliding down the ramp.

One by one the souls stiffened in their cages. Arms and leg jutted out through the bars. The soul within the bars beneath me craned his neck. His eyes, nostrils, and mouths lit up.

Satan scooped Pan up and lifted him to face him.

The congregation of souls spoke as one. "WE FOUND YOU."

The great horned god looked like a mosquito in Satan's palm.

Pan stood on an eyeball as big as a hot air balloon. He tried to dig his claws into the collagen surface before Satan closed his hand into a fist.

I didn't want to stick around to see how this played out.

"I'll let you two to break the ice."

The soul in the cage beneath me tilted his head back to cast his glowing eyes upon me.

"COME CLOSER." The collective called.

"I don't want to be a third wheel."

It hadn't occurred to me that Satan's mouthpieces could hear me too.

"COME CLOSER."

"Yeah…I'm out."

"CLOSER."

I climbed around the cage until I spotted the archway I'd entered from. At this point it was a hole in the wall. The platform beneath it was gone, slanted into the rest of the ramp. The only way I'd make it back to the Oralia was if I flew in.

Worse still, it was a 30-foot drop between here and there. I traced the fall from the cobblestones to the cauldron, from ramp to the four-headed titan. Then I remembered the lump weighing my coat down.

I gripped the bars with one hand, unbuckled my coat with the other, and reached into my pocket. I uncoiled the sex swing, and shook out the knots and pulled the cord up. I latched the hooks to the cage, positioned the seat beneath me, and gripped the vines tight.

I took a deep breath, exhaled, and let go. Torches streaked through my vision. The archway grew closer, the line tightened, and I bungeed backward.

I straightened my legs as the swing swooped back down. The archway grew closer. I let go and rolled across the cobblestones; end over end until every muscle, every limb, every nook and cranny of me got hit with something. When I came to a complete stop I took a moment to reacquaint myself with solid ground. One deep breath and I was up again, prying a torch off the wall.

Satan's attention was fixed on the creature in his fist, but it wouldn't be long until it was back on me.

NO TIME TO REFLECT

I RAN into the torture chamber to find it trashed. I tripped over a pair of discarded shackles, swerved to avoid an upended iron maiden, and accidently drove my torch into the shattered remains of a Catherine wheel. There was no sense in trying to pry it out. The room had gotten real bright real fast. There were no windows, fans, or vents. It wasn't long before the smoke reached the ceiling.

I got low, covered my mouth, and crawled for the door.

Voices echoed from the cathedral. Satan's monotone congregation chanted as one. I couldn't tell what tongue their speech was in.

The smoke billowed to the floor, making it impossible to tell where I was going.

When I saw a sliver of light, I wrenched myself up, and hurled myself at the door. It burst open and the backdraft roared behind me. I staggered across the downed condom dispenser, crawled onto the carpet, and spotted a fire extinguisher. I scooped it from the floor to have some kind of weapon.

When I turned around the door was gone. It was hidden

behind the dispenser, which had stood back up entirely on its own.

I was almost relieved when I found hoof prints, drywall, and splinters scattered down the hall. The mess meant that this was really happening and I wasn't just a crazy woman with a fire extinguisher.

I held the nozzle up like the barrel of gun and peeked around the corner for the elevator. All clear.

I came around and punched the call button.

I said a prayer for every floor number. "Please don't be like I wrote it. Please don't be like I wrote it. Please don't be like I wrote it." I had the nozzle up preparing to blast whatever crawled out from the abyss.

The elevator dinged. The doors opened to the familiar grid of mirrors. I exhaled. Whatever parallel dimension housed the ninth cast of Rodin's *Gates of Hell*, the infinite elevator, and the M.C. Escher's stairs, I wasn't there anymore. This was a dimension that had yet to be written.

I stepped inside and pushed the button for the lobby, and dropped the extinguisher.

The doors shut reflecting an infinite hallway of frizzy haired faces looking every bit as crazy as the situation we'd come from.

"Mirror mirror on the wall..." I huffed. How did Stephen's poem go again?

I wrung the sweat out of my hair, wiped the ash off my brow, and checked my arms for cuts. I had almost caught my breath when the elevator stopped, the fluorescents flickered, and the neon grid did the same.

In the reflection, I noticed something moving and that word *crystallomancy came to me again.*

At first I thought it was a fly on the mirror, but when I scratched the surface the thing kept moving. It seemed impossible, but something was approaching from the vanishing point, right where all the reflections converged. A black dot came over the horizon, grew arms, legs, and horns.

He was far down the infinite hallway, but there was no mistaking the silhouette. In Pan vs. Satan, it never occurred to me that Pan might pull out a win. The horned god had been leeching off of Satan's mojo for two millennia it must have evened the odds between them.

I spun around to find Pan charging at me from all directions. The elevator compartments shook under his weight. The neon lines bobbed up and down breaking from the grid. The rules governing the geometry of mirror images weren't working. Pan presence broke the illusion.

The infinite hallway got more and more finite as he went.

Pan built up speed, vaulting over the elevator railings like hurdles. His hooves thundered down the mirrored mile, cracking the glass as they fell. His eyes streaked from room to room, leaving chart-like trails as he went.

I grabbed the fire extinguisher off the floor.

Pan ran with purpose. One hand swung at his side while the other slapped my reflections. One hoof touched down while the other vaulted for the next room. I spun around. All four Pans, on the horizontal plane, lowered their heads to ram me at once.

I raised the extinguisher and slammed it against the glass. The impact made a few measly cracks and I fell on my ass. I got back on my feet, raised it again this time charged from the opposite end of the elevator. I gave the next pass a running start, an extra grunt, and put all my weight on it. Cracks spread across the glass.

I turned around to find the infinite hallway remained.

"That's not how mirrors work!"

It didn't matter that the mirror on the opposite side was broken. That didn't stop Pan from charging from the other directions. I raised the extinguisher straight up and brought it down like a hammer.

Pan howled. I looked over my shoulder to find him huffing and puffing, eyes blazing, and teeth gnashing. He kept coming and I kept smashing, until the air twinkled, the walls were rubble, and the floor was covered in glass.

The handle broke off the extinguisher on its final downward swing. It bounced off the wall and I caught it out of instinct. That's when it occurred to me to look up. Pan fell through the tower of mirrors, with his arms out and his hooves pointed downward.

Screaming, I launched that fire extinguisher into orbit.

There was an explosion of glass and a hard and heavy impact. Everything went black.

•••

When I came to I was still seeing double. There was a throbbing sensation on one side of my noggin. The hooves hadn't gotten me, but the fire extinguisher had. The damn thing rolled down a mountain of glass.

I looked back up to find Pan's lifeless limbs dangling, severed at the waist, hanging by a tendon. I coughed a fist full of glass particles just as the tissue snapped. Pan's legs collapsed and blood showered from the gap. Viscera dripped through my vision. By the time I wiped my eyes to hit the DOOR OPEN button my reflection looked like a seagull in an oil spill.

ALL THAT GLITTERS IS NOT GOLD

THE ELEVATOR LET out sick little chime as the doors screeched open. The fire extinguisher rolled over the threshold, hitting a pair of familiar patent leather pumps, Pradas if I wasn't mistaken.

"So that's where he ran off to." The owner of those pumps muttered, sounding like she was regarding a lost puppy and not the severed limbs of a fallen god.

I looked up and saw Matilda.

She found me slouched over, hands trembling, shards rolling off my back into a pile at my ankles. My face was frozen, mouth hanging open, teeth chattering, eyes refusing to blink.

Matilda flashed the kind of nervous smile one might give for spoiling a surprise party. "So, this is awkward."

I opened my mouth not yet knowing what to say.

"I owe you an apology." Matilda traced the threshold of the elevator. "It wasn't supposed to go down like this."

I felt too disoriented, too woozy to say anything. I rubbed my temples to ease the dizziness instead. The elevator was already started to stink.

"I had to bait him out of his cave. I figured once we got him in the open trapping him would be easy." She pointed to the hole in the ceiling. "But he put up a fight. You wouldn't know to look at me but I'm still recovering myself."

I sneezed viscera, almost blacked out again, and found myself slapping my blood-spattered cheeks. Try as I might I couldn't shake the feeling of being punch drunk.

"Huh?"

"I was congratulating you on doing something Barkley never could." Matilda eyed Pan's splayed remains the way athletes stare at trophies. "Barkley's fine, by the way. He has a heightened resilience for these sorts of encounters, all my elite clients do. He's limping down the fire stairs as we speak."

Members of the hotel staff walked past, never thinking to inspect the source of that loud crashing sound. Their eyes shone red, like people in old flash photographs.

I had no clue what to make of any of this, so I kept my poker face up.

Matilda smirked, checked the left side of my face for cracks then moved onto the right. "Not so talkative tonight?" She put a hand up, indicating that the observation wasn't a challenge. "You've been through an ordeal. This would've been easier if you'd stayed with us. I'd have caught you before you fell into the cauldron."

"You've got to be kidding me."

Matilda stretched out on the frame of the elevator like a pinup model. "Oh don't look so surprised. Come on you knew it was me."

I couldn't help but steal another glance at her patent leather pumps.

"So the Devil really does where Prada."

Matilda kicked a heel up. "Great book. Adequate adaptation, but what can I say? It piqued my interest at the mere mention of my name."

I cocked my head. "So *she* has many names?"

Matilda snickered. "Oh please. I am so over gender. It's a binary construct by an uninspired author. You'd all be better off casting your genitals into the fire."

She offered her hand and I took it without thinking. She stepped forward rather than pull me out.

She put her hand on my shoulder. "As much as this décor suites me I imagine you'd prefer to continue this discussion someplace else."

•••

And with a snap of a finger we were back at the bar, in the same spots as last time.

The bartender was pouring Champagne into a tower of glasses, as though he'd been anticipating our arrival. There was an empty glare in his eyes, like the staff in the lobby. He wasn't startled when a pair of strange women materialized in front of him.

Matilda took a glass off the top of the tower and downed all of it in a single sip. She tossed it over her shoulder and it shattered on the floor.

Matilda helped herself to two more glasses. "Garçon. You can add these to my tab."

The bartender spoke without looking in Matilda direction. "But ma'am your money is no good here."

Matilda wiped her lips and flung her glasses over her shoulder. "I know. I just like to say it."

I reached for a glass to find my hand was cleansed of the viscera that was coating it. Weirder still, I was wearing an emerald cocktail dress. I felt along my forehead. The bump was still there.

Matilda waved me along. "Go on. It's Champagne. It's your favorite."

I set the glass back in the tower. "I think I've had enough."

I leaned back in the stool and lost myself in a maze-like pattern on the ceiling. When I looked back down Matilda was running her armored ring along the handle of the attaché case. Talk about déjà vu.

Maybe it was a concussion or maybe I was still dreaming, but the art deco architecture appeared to be moving. Line patterns flowed into the angles and back out again. The shoulders of the gargoyles rose and fell, like those granite beasts were breathing.

"Nope, Noelle. This is not a dream." Matilda said with amusement.

"What is this place?"

Matilda shrugged. "The Oralia? One of many façades I've designed for one reason or another."

"A façade?"

"An idea I put out into the world, much like Barkley's writing career, it seems legitimate on the surface, but it isn't."

I never imagined a conversation with the devil would devolve into celebrity gossip, but here we were.

"Barkley didn't write *any* of his books, did he?"

Matilda leaned forward like she gave a toss about secrets here. "Oh Barkley knew how to pitch his stories, writing them, not so much, but what he lacked in talent he made up for by networking, which lead him to me. So I made him an offer: fame, fortune, and everlasting life for a modest price."

"His soul?" I widened my eyes, mocking the gravity of the cost. "Too bad you didn't live up to your end of the bargain."

Matilda shook her head. "Oh, but I did. I granted all of his wishes. I just couldn't give him talent. So I found a workaround."

"Ghostwriters?"

Matilda nodded. "With you I won't have to. Never mind what I said on the phone. Girl, you've got the goods, but it would be a shame to let your talent go to waste in this market place."

I crossed my arms. "And my soul is what, just the price of doing business? Kind of cliché, don't you think?"

"As a writer you should learn the difference between what makes something a cliché and what makes it a classic."

"Well eternal suffering has never really been my thing."

"Mine either, but that's not how it works." Matilda rolled her manicured hands through the air. "I mean what is a soul really? It's just energy. When it goes it doesn't take your personality with it. It doesn't keep you connected to your friends or family. When you die, no matter what you do, your memories, everything that makes you *you*, ends up being worm food. I want to keep you alive so we can have fun working together."

I pointed to the ceiling. "Those souls upstairs might beg to differ."

Matilda scanned her brow as though she hadn't a clue what I was talking about and then smiled abruptly. "Oh they're not dead. They just failed to honor their agreements. They're in the penalty box until I need them again."

I raised my eyebrow. "That's kind of a deterrent."

Matilda nodded matter of factly. "As long as you pick up when I need a favor you'll be free and clear to indulge in all of life's pleasures."

Matilda pointed in the vague direction of the elevator.

"That counts as a big one. It'll be a while before I call you again. In the meantime, I'll get you published, have all the major studios bidding on your work, and schedule you for Ted talks about women in genre fiction. That sure beats retail and ramen. Don't you think?"

I nodded. It did, even with the hidden fees, it did.

Matilda shifted her head from shoulder to shoulder. She could see through my poker face and now she knew she'd piqued my interest. "So what do you say? Are you ready to live the life you deserve, to be admired, and have a whole fleet of bellboys at your beck and call?"

I couldn't help but nod. Of course I was ready for something better, but I couldn't help but wonder. "Was Stephen one of yours?"

Matilda rolled her eyes. "I'm much less selective with who I hire to tend my façade as I am with whom I offer immortality to."

"Was he entranced when we?"

"Consummated your blessed union? Not by me."

I sighed, happy to know that at least my awkward interactions with him were real. I had enough trust issues without adding another to the pile.

Matilda snapped her fingers and a document appeared in her fingers. She slipped it over and a pen appeared my hand.

Matilda smiled. "Now *this* is not a non-disclosure agreement."

No it was not. This contract was hand written on aged parchment. The material reminded me of the banners in the cathedral and the ink was the color of rust.

Weirder still, there was something odd about the proportions of the lettering. The relationship between the calligraphy, the spacing, and the layout had a hypnotic effect. The words seemed to breathe, like poetry on a ribcage.

Trying to grasp the text was like trying to read in a dream. The words dissolved before I could absorb them. They weren't for mortal minds to comprehend, but I knew that Matilda's offer was true. I was certain she could deliver fame, fortune, and eternal youth. I felt that in my bones.

All I had to do was sign on the dotted line.

Matilda's eyes widened when I focused on the pen. She rubbed her hands together. "Write your stories with all the meta references and forth wall breaking you want. Don't worry if dullards at the airport get it or not. Don't worry if anyone thinks you're likable. I'm the tastemaker. I say what goes."

I stared at the contract until I felt like I was going to fall into the fine print. *COME CLOSER...CLOSER...CLOSER STILL.*

I leaned forward and stared into the eyes of the devil. I saw the same thing I saw in every producer who thought his cruelty was some kind of favor. I saw the same dumb lust. I saw the certainty that the world functioned on greed. I saw myself reflected back as a product to be packaged, an object pretending to be a person.

I dropped the pen. "No."

There was a spark of pain in Matilda's soulless eyes.

"No?"

"No."

"You'll never get published, you will never have anything you want."

"I'll self-publish."

"That's its own hell."

"It beats the alternative."

"It will wear you down."

"I don't know. Something about learning all this paranormal shit is real is kind of inspiring."

Matilda sighed. "I'll give you your own imprint. You can lift female horror writers out of obscurity. Be the force for change this industry needs-"

She cut herself off. She could see it in my eyes. She had nothing to bargain with. She couldn't afford me anymore.

Matilda gave me an uncharacteristically sympathetic smile. "I like you. I really do. You're one of my favorites. This will happen some day. You just don't know it."

"No, it won't."

Matilda sighed, got up and smoothed her jacket. She gave

me her hand and I let her help me up. "The offer will always be open when you change your mind."

This time Matilda didn't leave through the revolving doors. She walked out of the bar, toward the checkout counter, then through it. The concierge didn't seem to notice. Matilda phased through the wall and disappeared.

The gargoyles leered at me from their perches on the ceiling, their claws digging into their stands, their nostrils flaring, their mouths watering. They were positioned to swoop down and maul me the moment my back was turned.

I raised my chin up. "You saw what happened to the last guy who messed with me. Do you really want some of that?"

The gargoyles went back to playing dead and I walked on.

"That's what I thought."

Then I did what I'd wanted to do since I'd entered the hotel.

I left.

I felt lighter with each step. I had no publisher, no contract, and no money, but I had a hell of a story.

I pressed on through the revolving doors and savored the air. It was dirty and full of smog and doubt, but it was real. This city was full of façades, just like the Oralia, each one promising to make my dreams come true. It was time to leave them all behind. It was time to make reality my bitch.

ABOUT THE AUTHOR

Drew Chial is a writer who haunts the coffee shops of Minneapolis Minnesota where he lives with his cat Nemo. He's been a board member of the *Minneapolis Screenwriter's Workshop* and a script reader for the production company *Werc Werk Works*. He's won the *Short Story and Flash Fiction Society's Flash Fiction Contest*. His articles have been featured on *Word Press's Freshly Pressed* page and *RogerEbert.com*. *The Fancy Pants Gangsters* produced an audio drama from his short story *The Narration* for the *Red Shift* podcast. His short story *Grieving in Reverse* was published in the collection *Walking Hand and Hand into Extinction: Stories Inspired By True Detective*. And he does not use ghostwriters...yet. Follow him on Twitter, IG & FB @DrewChial & drewchialauthor.com

ALSO BY CLASH BOOKS

TRAGEDY QUEENS: STORIES INSPIRED BY LANA DEL REY & SYLVIA PLATH

edited by Leza Cantoral

DARK MOONS RISING IN A STARLESS NIGHT

Mame Bougouma Diene

NOHO GLOAMING & THE CURIOUS CODA OF ANTHONY SANTOS

Daniel Knauf (Creator of HBO's Carnivàle)

IF YOU DIED TOMORROW I WOULD EAT YOUR CORPSE

Wrath James White

GIRL LIKE A BOMB

Autumn Christian

THE ANARCHIST KOSHER COOKBOOK

Maxwell Bauman

HORROR FILM POEMS

Christoph Paul

NIGHTMARES IN ECTASY

Brendan Vidito

THE VERY INEFFECTIVE HAUNTED HOUSE

Jeff Burk

CENOTE CITY

Monique Quintana

THIS BOOK AIN'T NUTTIN TO FUCK WITH: A WU-TANG TRIBUTE ANTHOLOGY

edited by Christoph Paul & Grant Wamack

www.ingramcontent.com/pod-product-compliance
Lightning Source LLC
Chambersburg PA
CBHW070503170726
48291CB00008B/2628

* 9 7 8 1 9 4 4 8 6 6 2 2 8 *